WHEN MICHAEL CALLS

When Michael Calls

John Farris

NEW ENGLISH LIBRARY
TIMES MIRROR

First published in the United States of America by Trident Press
Copyright © 1967 by John Farris

*

SPECIALLY ABRIDGED NEL EDITION MAY 1970
Reprinted June 1970

*

NEL Books are published by
New English Library Limited from Barnard's Inn, Holborn, London E.C.1.
Made and printed in Great Britain by Hunt Barnard Printing Ltd., Aylesbury, Bucks.

4500514 3

One

THE YELLOW SHADES COUNTY SCHOOL BUS DROPPED PEGGY Connelly and two other second-graders off at the corner and Peggy walked the rest of the way atop the low stone wall that separated the Connelly property from the street, taking care not to scuff her good school shoes. A tall young man was digging in the front yard and Peggy paused for a few moments near the white gate in the wall. Peggy didn't particularly like Randle and avoided him whenever possible, but she couldn't resist a freshly dug hole, so she hopped down and walked through the scattered leaves to where he was working.

"What is that going to be?" Peggy asked.

Without looking around, Harry Randle unloaded a shovelful of dirt very close to her new shoes, but Peggy was ready for that and she didn't flinch. Instead she looked up at him in her peculiarly rapt and courteous way, willing as always to respond to any indication of goodwill.

Randle leaned his shovel against a wrought-iron signpost and wiped his perspiring forehead with the back of one hand. He smiled then, not really looking at her.

"It's for your dead cat," he said.

"I don't have a dead cat."

"I wouldn't be that sure."

"I'm sure; I don't. Do you mean Satch?"

Harry Randle didn't reply. He wasn't much older than some of the high school boys, as far as Peggy could tell, but he was a lot meaner. His remarks about her cat, even though she knew better than to believe him, worried her, so she looked here and there in the yard, hoping to find Satch in the best of health. Then she glanced toward the street, where Dr. Britton's station wagon was parked. She saw two wrapped evergreen shrubs in the back.

"*That's* what you're doing," Peggy said. "You're digging

holes for the plants."

Randle lifted his shovel and jabbed it casually into the ground a few times, still smiling. "Dead cat makes good plant food, makes 'em *grow*."

"You're a faker. You wouldn't touch Satch."

"Better make sure he doesn't come around me again," Randle said seriously. "I almost got him last time." He lashed out with his shovel, smacking the flat blade against the ground. "Ha!"

Peggy edged closer to the hole, peered inside. Satisfied that it was empty, she started toward the house. Harry Randle was one of the doctor's regular hands on his farm, but he came over to the Connellys' once a week to do yard work and other chores Helen Connelly couldn't do herself. Peggy had long ago given up trying to be friends with Randle. Apparently he just didn't like little girls, something new in her experience.

Near the porch Peggy became aware that Randle was quietly following her and she turned quickly, frowning; but he wasn't up to anything.

"What are you jumping for?" he said, enjoying her discomfort. "As long as you're going inside, tell Dr. Britton I have to walk down to the Texaco station and pick up my car. I'll be back in a few minutes."

"OK," Peggy said, and she walked on unhurriedly to the glassed-in front porch of the two-story frame house. Her mother kept a few items on the porch—unwieldy spinning wheels and cider presses and occasionally a full-size wood-burning stove—but the porch wasn't cluttered. Unlike a lot of the antique dealers in The Shades, Helen Connelly had a real shop, not just a junk emporium.

The foyer, living room and what had been a sun porch on the north side of the house were now filled with antiques. Peggy walked through the foyer—passing two display cases containing irresistible pieces of jewelry which she sometimes was allowed to touch, under supervision—dropped her school things on the stairway and entered the kitchen, which took up most of the rear of the first floor. Her mother was there, having coffee with Elsa and Andrew Britton.

"I hope it's going to turn *cold* tonight," Peggy said. "I'm tired of this hot weather." She began rummaging in the breadbox.

"I'm frying doughnuts here, 'less you're too impatient," said

6

Brenda, the cook.

"I thought you had some fried already."

"A little cool weather and we won't be able to stir the tourists with a stick," Elsa Britton remarked sadly.

"Them doughnuts is still hot, Peggy; don't cry to me when you burn your mouth."

"Peggy, don't eat standing up," Helen said to her daughter.

"Dr. Britton, do you have any bees in your car?"

The doctor smiled. "Matter of fact, I picked up a shipment of bees, with queen, at the post office this afternoon—"

"How many?"

"I'd say there should be about fifteen thousand in the hive this time of the year."

Peggy sat down beside her mother and looked at him, enraptured. "What are you going to do with so many bees?"

"I'm going to train some of them."

Peggy was puzzled by the concept of trained bees. "Can I watch?"

"Sure, come over any time."

"Bees, Andy?" Helen said doubtfully.

"Perfectly safe," he assured her.

"What about that boy in Springfield who died from a bee sting this summer?"

"He was probably hypoallergic."

Peggy nodded thoughtfully. "Did you ever get stung?"

"Plenty of times."

"You'd better train the new bees not to bite, then," she advised him.

The telephone in the hall rang.

"That's Rosalind!" Peggy said.

"What'll I tell her?" Helen asked over one shoulder as she left the kitchen to answer the phone.

"Oh, tell her I'll be *delayed*."

"Right," Helen said. She frowned at the school things piled on the stairs and picked up the receiver of the telephone, which was sitting on a meticulously refinished Sheraton table at the entrance to the living room.

"Auntie Helen?"

She was looking through the glass to the right of the door, looking beyond the porch at the yard, where Randle had left his shovel leaning against the sign that read "HELEN CONNELLY—ANTIQUES," and at first she wasn't certain just what she'd heard.

"Yes . . . hello ? Is that you, Rosalind ?"

"Auntie Helen . . ." She frowned; not a girl's voice. "Auntie Helen, I missed the school bus. Will you come get me ?"

Wrong Number, she thought. "Who is this ?"

"It's Michael, Auntie Helen."

"What ?"

"It's Michael."

Helen said nothing at all.

"Are you coming ?"

"Just . . . a minute. Now, who *is* this ?" But the connection was broken before she finished.

For several moments she continued to hold the receiver, her eyes fixed on the yard, on the street. A couple of kids went by on bicycles. Far away the ridges were a mass of yellow leaves, ripe for a stunning autumn show. The sky was blue and filled with lumbering clouds, and the sun blazed long shadows everywhere.

"OK," she said, half to herself, then replaced the receiver and went back to the kitchen.

"Did you tell Rosalind ?"

"It wasn't Rosalind, sweetie." She sat down and stared at her half-empty coffee cup, then out the back door.

"You don't look too happy, Helen," Dr. Britton said.

"I just had a—" Her expression froze and she glanced quickly at her daughter, who apparently wasn't listening, but she went on in a more cautious tone of voice. "You know, one of those calls."

"Crank call ?"

"Ah!" Elsa said, darkly, as if she were still thinking of artists and folk singers.

"No—I mean, that's not it exactly, Andy. I suppose it was just some sort of juvenile prank. It was a boy—about ten years old, I guess."

"What did he say to you ?" Elsa demanded.

"He said—" Helen's mouth twisted in a bemused, half-sheepish way. "He said he wanted to be picked up. He was down at the school and he'd missed his bus, and he wanted me—"

"Is that all ?" Elsa seemed disappointed. "You looked snakebit."

"In a way it was . . . cruel, because he, whoever that was, said he was Michael."

8

"Michael?" Dr. Britton repeated, and Brenda looked up from the stove.

"Michael."

Two

LIKE NINETY PERCENT OF THE PEOPLE WHO LIVED IN THE SHADES, Helen Connelly was not a native of the area. Neither was she a "year-arounder," which was Elsa Britton's term for all recent settlers who were attracted by the carefully preserved wilderness and by the lively artists' colony. Helen had been a Chicagoan and a debutante, and at twenty she'd had a West Point chapel wedding. Not quite a year later, her husband, who was the number-three man in his class, died aboard a torpedoed troop ship bound for North Africa.

She had spent the wartime years in Washington and the years immediately following in New York, working at a succession of "interesting" and "challenging" jobs, and it was a puzzle to her family and friends why she didn't remarry. To her earnest suitors she gave the easy and the obvious answer.

Months had passed before she began to doubt her reasoning, to attack her complacency and the carefully wrought illusions that had kept her alive and functioning for so long. In her mind she had preserved the precious, irreplaceable marriage in infinite detail, as if he might return at any moment. Was it wrong to cling to that beautiful year, was it cowardly? He will not come back, she told herself boldly. But she knew that, she knew it . . . and quite abruptly one winter afternoon she realized the truth, with a feeling of suffocation, of horror.

The months that followed had been harrowing, but through plain neglect the one-and-only marriage had dwindled to a proper distance in her thoughts, and after that, falling in love had been easy and natural. First she fell in love with The Shades itself, and then, much later, with Ed Connelly.

They were driving back from the post office in the village of

The Shades when Peggy said, "Who's Michael, Mother ?"

Helen was used to questions out of nowhere but she was sure she looked a little surprised at this one because Peggy said patiently, "The boy who called you a little while ago."

"Oh." Helen stopped at the state highway intersection, then continued on up White Church Road. "I don't really know who that was, Peggy; some little boy who should have better things to do than annoy people over the telephone."

"But you said it was Michael. Michael who ?"

Helen hesitated, then explained with a smile, "Michael was your uncle Craig's brother, honey, but he died a long time ago. Before you were born. Uncle Craig was only eleven years old then."

"What happened to Michael ?"

"He ran—ran away from home often, and the last time he ran away he got lost in a blizzard."

"Didn't anybody ever find him ?"

"Yes, but it was weeks and weeks afterward." Helen pulled up in front of the house, parked her ranch wagon on the asphalt pavement which she'd provided for her customers and took the key out of the ignition. "So you see that wasn't Michael—my nephew Michael—on the telephone today. It was someone pretending to be." Helen was prepared for a thornier job of explaining but Peggy confounded her by dropping the subject.

On weekdays during the fall season it was unusual for more than a dozen people to stop and browse and, as a rule, Helen closed her shop after two o'clock. But on this afternoon she had a late appointment with an old customer who collected milk glass, and while Helen was entertaining her, a car from Illinois pulled up and several elderly tourists asked if they could look around. They stayed until past dark and bought nothing, which was no surprise.

So that was that. Helen washed her hands in the lavatory under the stairs and went happily to supper, which Brenda had been keeping hot for the past ten minutes.

Peggy was making a mound of her turnips to one side of her plate and discussing the ramifications of her latest falling out with Rosalind, who was Peggy's best friend when she wasn't being such a terrible baby, when the telephone rang again. Helen went to answer, noticing that it seemed colder in the house, as if the temperature outside was plunging.

"Hello ?"

"Auntie Helen?"

Oh, God, she thought involuntarily, wincing, but she gained control of herself and said sharply, "I don't know why you think this is funny, but I'm not impressed and I want you to *stop calling here*. Do you understand?"

"Auntie Helen, why didn't you pick me up?" the voice said plaintively.

"Now, listen—"

"It's dark, and I can't walk home. My mother's going to be mad—"

"Who is this?"

There was no reply, but Helen heard a kind of sighing on the line that caused the skin of her forearms to tighten until she tentatively identified the sound as wind. She glanced outside and saw leaves flying through the nimbus of light from the lantern outside her gate.

"Please come," the boy said, and he sounded subdued, doleful. "What's wrong, Auntie Helen? Are you mad at me?"

"I'm not—" she started to say, but the connection was broken suddenly, as it had been earlier that day. Helen rubbed her forehead with her index finger, listening is if she half expected to hear the voice again despite the steady and familiar signal on the line; she put the receiver down unnecessarily hard.

"Now I'm getting mad," she said aloud, confirming it for herself, and Peggy called from the kitchen.

"Who was that, Mother?"

"A spook," Helen muttered, stopping to make an adjustment of the thermostat before she entered the kitchen. "Baby, are you warm enough in that sweater?"

"Yes," Peggy said. "What spook?"

Helen went to the stove to pour more coffee for herself. "That's just an expression. By spook I mean . . . a child who gets on people's nerves."

Twice before eight o'clock the telephone rang; each time she tightened up and struggled with feelings of dismay and anger before answering. But neither of the callers was "Michael."

Peggy went to bed a little later than usual, and for an hour afterward she was restless because of the pane-rattling, frost-bringing wind that roared through the narrows of the valley and poured leaves upon their roof. Once her daughter had settled down for good, Helen holed up in the office nook which she had outfitted with a rolltop desk and gradually, over the years, crammed with all the treasures she had found it impossible to part with.

About eleven the phone rang again, startling her. She had been absorbed in an expensive, beautifully photographed study of antebellum Louisiana mansions which a friend had loaned to her, and the wind had lulled her into a series of yawns. Helen sat up straight, and a dark bust of a child caught her eye.

"Time for all good little boys to be asleep," she said, looking again at the pendulum clock on the wall opposite her desk to check the time. And she felt a little worried, not because it might be the same boy calling again, but because she was automatically assuming, whenever the telephone rang, that it *was* him.

After all, he'd had his fun.

Yes, but, she thought, and hurried across the foyer to lift the receiver before Peggy woke up.

She heard someone crying.

You've had your fun, Helen tried to say, but she couldn't; her mouth had dried up.

He was weeping this time, heartbroken, and his sobs shocked her because it wasn't a child playacting; she was certain of that. He was terrified, helpless, alone.

"Auntie Helen—"

"Y-yes—"

"I'm . . . home . . . and there's . . . nobody . . . here."

"Oh, my God," Helen said quickly and harshly, "don't keep this up. Whoever you are, please—"

"There's . . . nobody here. Where's my mother?"

The wind outside, to which she had paid little attention for the last hour, suddenly turned on the house and thumped at the door. Helen fell back against the table, trembling.

"Where's *Craig?* Where's my brother?"

"Please," Helen whispered. "What are you trying to do?"

He was weeping again. She put the receiver down on the table and ran from it, into the kitchen. But the blackness outside the windows was too forbidding; she couldn't stay there. And it seemed she hadn't escaped him after all; she was still trembling, still vulnerable, and pathetically frightened for a mature woman who was sure that she knew a great deal about the foibles of children.

Yes, real children. But this one is a sadistic, depressing ogre.

12

When Helen felt she could breathe normally, she returned to the foyer and picked up the receiver of the telephone. She heard nothing this time except the sighing, the tricky fade and rise of the wind, somewhere.

I'm going to be rid of you, she thought. *I'm going to stop you if it takes*—"Hello," she said, and paused. "You wanted to talk to me. That's a good idea. I certainly want to talk to you." Again Helen paused. "I know you're still there, so why don't you say something? How long do you think—"

He screamed then, not in her ear but seemingly from a distance, and Helen cringed.

"Michael!" she said, not meaning to. "Mi—"

"I'm dead, aren't I? I'm dead, I'm *dead!*"

She hung up instantly, and seconds later tears formed in her eyes.

"Mother?" Peggy called from her room.

"Wha—what is it, Peg?"

"Who are you talking to?"

"I'm sorry if I woke you up. Please go back to sleep. It was only . . . Reverend Bartlett. I was talking to him on the phone."

"You sounded loud."

"Yes. I'm sorry, baby. Good night."

"Good night."

Loud enough to wake Peggy, she thought, despairingly. Her heart still felt flogged and sore. This thing is really getting to me, and I'm going to have to—*It wasn't Michael.*

She looked up, startled by the denial that had so abruptly crossed her mind.

Of course it wasn't Michael, and I'm not haunted.

But I could use someone to talk to, Helen admitted bleakly, and reached for a brass box of cigarettes on the table beside the telephone.

While she was dialing she felt as if she might be surrendering something valuable of herself, surrendering self-reliance perhaps. She and Peggy had lived in their house, alone, since the death of Ed Connelly, and not once during those years had she given in to the need to call someone during a particularly lonely and difficult evening, to invite company. But this time—

Morning seemed a long way off, and she was too disturbed by the calls from "Michael" to wait that long to discuss them with a friend.

"Craig? I hate to bother you this time of night, but . . .

You're not? Good. I'm afraid I have a—an odd sort of thing has happened here tonight and . . . Could you? Oh, I'd appreciate . . . No, don't come barreling down that road; it's not all that urgent."

Helen was surprised to feel considerably relieved after saying good-bye to her nephew. To hell with all that self-reliance, she thought cheerfully, and went into the kitchen to make coffee.

Craig Young was twenty-eight, which is not extremely youthful for a practicing psychologist, and many men have begun to mature strikingly near thirty, but to Craig's occasional chagrin he still looked very much like a college freshman.

"Whoever the boy is," Craig said, after pouring his third cup of coffee, "it's obvious that he knows a lot about Michael, and about us."

"Too much."

"I suppose some of the people around here still talk about my mother, and Michael. Any impressionable kid has fantasies of running away and dying in a—well, in a romantic way far from home, so it's reasonable to assume your caller has let the whole story of the Youngs get the best of him."

"He's more than just an ordinary impressionable boy. He's fantastic, Craig."

"How do you mean?"

"He's convinced that he *is* Michael. Because what I heard over the telephone wasn't make-believe. He wasn't acting. Everything he said was pathetically real. And the way he sobbed!" Helen shook her head. "I wish I could remember the quality of Michael's voice . . ."

Craig tilted his chair back and smiled skeptically. "All ten-year-old boys tend to sound alike on the telephone. You're not hinting we have a ghost on our hands, are you?"

"He called me Auntie Helen," she replied, looking no less troubled than when Craig had walked in.

"So did I, while I was growing up."

"Oh, no," Helen said quickly. "You didn't. That was Michael. Only Michael. I'll have to admit our pretender has frightened me, but disregarding his ability and his motives for the moment, how could he possibly know to call me *Auntie* Helen?"

Craig thought about it, then spread his hands and grinned broadly. "All right, I'm stumped. But there *is* an explanation."

14

"Hmm," she said, unconsoled.

"I deal with troubled children; they've been my major interest in life for going on six years now. You're bewildered by this impostor who keeps calling you up and scaring the— And I don't blame you, but: bear in mind he is an impostor, and he'll get tired of his game, and take up something else. Sex, I hope."

"When will he get tired?"

"I don't know. I'm sorry to say, the more absorbed they are in their game, the more persistent they can be; speaking professionally, it sometimes takes months, or years, to separate a disturbed child from his fantasies and delusions."

Helen put her hands over her face, and groaned.

Craig stretched and got up to put his saucer and cup in the sink. "Want me to stick around tonight?"

"What? Oh, that's not necessary." Her eyes went to the stove clock and she stood up hurriedly. "I'm sorry, Craig. Twenty minutes to one—why didn't you shut me up half an hour ago?"

"Enjoyed it. Haven't been over for quite a while."

"How's Amy?"

"She's been away visiting her folks. I think she got back tonight."

"We're going to have an evening meal soon," Helen promised, walking him to the front door.

Craig picked up his shearling coat on the way and put it on, yawning. "That wind's not going to quit till morning. Sometimes I think it'll blow me right off Ben Lomond. Tell Peg I'm sorry I didn't get to see her."

Helen went as far as the front porch with him, and waited outside, shivering, as he walked to the gate.

Inside, the telephone rang, but at first she didn't hear it because of the wind. When she did become aware of the telephone she started inside, changed her mind and yelled, "Craig!"

He looked up as he was about to get into his car.

"Telephone!" she said, pointing, and ran to answer.

Craig hesitated, then shut the car door and hurried back to the house. But Helen had let the door close behind her. He tried the knob and found that the door was locked. Then he considered ringing the bell, and quickly thought better of it. He peered in through the narrow glass to the left of the door.

15

The foyer was dark but he could see her, standing at the edge of light from the kitchen, one hand on the table, the other holding the receiver of the telephone to her ear.

He rapped on the glass. "Helen!"

She turned and put down the receiver and came. When she opened the door her face was chalk, her eyes blank.

"That boy again?" he said, scowling.

"Yes, it was Michael."

"What? Now listen, Helen, you can't . . ." He took her arm and turned her from the doorway, entered the house himself. With the wind shut out, Craig could speak more quietly.

"Aunt Helen, that's not Michael, my brother Michael, who's calling you. Don't let yourself get in the habit of—" He stopped because she was paying no attention to him. "What did he say this time?" He gripped her arm more tightly and she responded with a wince.

"Oh, Craig, that hurts me!"

"I'm sorry," he apologized, letting go. "But you looked—"

"Don't worry, I'm really all right. This time he just—he said some things that—"

"What, Helen?"

"His voice was altogether different. So terribly cold. He— I think I want to sit down, if you don't mind." She went into the office and slumped in front of her desk while Craig filled the doorway.

"He couldn't have had much to say. You were only on the phone about half a minute."

Helen lifted her eyes. "All he said was, 'My mother's dead, isn't she? Why did you send her away to die, Auntie Helen?' "

Craig was silent for half a minute, looking bleakly at her. He said finally, "This is one I'd like to write up, if we ever get hold of the lad who's making the calls. I suppose . . . I'd better notify the sheriff."

"What good will that do?"

"Well . . ." Craig shrugged, then admitted, "No good at all, I'm sure. I was hoping it might make you feel a little better."

"Good Lord, Craig, I'm not that upset!" After a moment she smiled, her face softening. "And I didn't mean to jump on you. I think I could use a good night's sleep."

"Before you go up, wrap the telephone in a thick towel and put it in the closet. If he's still in a talkative mood this late, let him wear his dialing finger out."

16

Helen nodded. "I know you can't predict how long this boy will keep calling, Craig. But do you think he'll . . . limit himself to calls?"

"What do you mean?"

"What if he gets the urge to—to come around?"

"I don't think that's likely, Helen."

"You can't be sure, can you?"

"Not without—"

"He was angry with me, Craig. He sounded betrayed." Helen stared at him, unable to keep the concern she felt from her face.

"Maybe . . . you and Peg should come up on the mountain with me for a few days if you don't feel safe here."

"That would mean a lot of explaining to Peg. So far she's not disturbed by the calls, and not more than normally curious. If Mi— If the boy keeps calling, I should be able to . . . Well, I think I'm prepared for almost anything; I'll just have to handle him the best way I can."

Craig said slowly, "I think there's a good chance you won't hear from him again. He more or less threatened you this last time and accused you of doing away with his mother." Helen looked startled and dismayed, but Craig went on, eagerly. "That's good; it may have been the key to the fantasy which he constructed from elements of our lives. He's a boy whose mother died, or left him without explanation. Now he has an explanation, and he's fixed the blame. He doesn't need his fantasy anymore; no matter how long it took him to become 'Michael,' he can discard 'Michael' in an instant."

Helen studied him rather dubiously. "You're the psychologist. Not just trying to cheer me up, are you?"

Craig smiled guilelessly. "It's a reasonable theory. I'll go home and kick it around, unless you'd rather have me stay—"

"No, go home, for heaven's sake. In another thirty seconds I'll be yawning in your face."

He bent to kiss her forehead, then walked into the wind, chin down. Helen ducked back inside, letting go the yawn she had threatened him with. She stayed downstairs just long enough to put out the lights, thinking about Craig's moustache and wondering how long it would be before Amy got him to shave it off; thinking about the dollar bet. All that Craig had surmised about the telephoning boy sounded logical. She was content to believe he was right, as she started up the stairs.

And the telephone rang.

Damn you!

Her jaw set, Helen snatched up the receiver.

"Hey, Bertram! Hey, old buddy!"

"Friend," Helen said, "thank you for having the wrong number."

Three

THE GREENLEAF SCHOOL WAS LOCATED A COUPLE OF MILES FROM the village center in an area which old settlers still referred to as Eveningshade: a hollow about half a mile long hemmed in by sometimes vertical ridges four hundred to a thousand feet high. As a rule it took a great deal of money to send a boy to the Greenleaf School for a year, but most of the parents who had sons at Greenleaf were sufficiently desperate not to care what it cost. In addition to topflight teachers experienced in dealing with bright but undisciplined children, there were also two psychiatrists and two clinical psychologists on the staff. Both psychiatrists commuted once a week from St. Louis, which was 140 miles away. Consequently Craig Young and his assistant, Amy Lawlor, did most of the work with the two dozen boys who required regular therapy.

They were having a late lunch in the faculty dining room when Craig mentioned the telephone calls his aunt had received the day before. Amy was immediately intrigued and pressed him for details.

"One of our gentlemen?" she suggested, when Craig had told her all he knew.

He packed his pipe with tobacco and lighted it, talking between puffs. "Helen thought so, but I couldn't go along with her. We've got missing-parent syndromes, all right. But I can't believe any of our boys have ever heard of my brother Michael. After all, that was sixteen years ago. Who still talks about him? *I* don't; I hardly think about Michael. I doubt if any of the locals remember him well; the story's not all that interesting."

"The boy who called Helen certainly knew a lot about Michael, and his fantasy was beautifully organized. Morbid too. If I were Helen I'd have climbed the walls."

Craig said cheerfully, "He hasn't called today, though; I was talking to Helen just before I came down to eat. So the hunch I had last night might be accurate: the boy doesn't need 'Michael' anymore, and he's dropped him."

"That's probably the answer," Amy said after thinking it over, "but your aunt was convinced that Michael was real."

"She didn't know what to think."

"Craig . . . you don't believe in spirits, but—"

"Damn right I don't."

"But," Amy said firmly, "I do."

Craig groaned, then smiled at her. "Nothing supernatural about this at all."

"Oh, no? I think we could build a strong case for the supernatural."

"Go ahead, build a case. Are you going to finish your pie?"

"Help yourself. Craig, you've assumed that the caller is a boy who has so familiarized himself with the story of your brother that he has actually come to believe he is Michael. But on the other hand you admit it's improbable that a boy who is, say, ten years of age could learn that much about another boy, dead for sixteen years."

"Improbable; not impossible."

"I'll concede that point. But this boy called Helen 'Auntie Helen,' and she swears no one but Michael Young ever called her that."

"Probably not less than a hundred people heard Mike say 'Auntie Helen' when he was alive."

"I won't concede there. It's not the sort of . . . verbal idiosyncrasy that's likely to be remembered."

Craig forked in the last of the cherry pie and looked at her indulgently. "What's your solution?"

"It could be that the spirit of your brother Michael—"

"Picked up the telephone and called Helen a few times. What telephone? Where? In that astral waiting room the occultists are always talking about?"

"If you just want to have a good laugh—"

"No, no, I'm sorry. I'm listening. Please tell me."

Amy sighed and decided she wasn't very angry, and smiled

slightly, but she was completely serious as she continued. "The spirit of your brother might be possessing another, outwardly normal boy here in The Shades. A boy with latent psychic-sensitive qualities."

"Demonic possession? If there *was* such a boy, it wouldn't be any secret. His parents would have brought him to us in a bag to have his demon exorcised, or whatever you do with demons."

"No. The boy I'm thinking of might be puzzling his parents by acting . . . differently; but it wouldn't be cause for alarm unless Michael, the spirit Michael, greatly upset his host, or made him do wild things. That's not what Michael wants, however. He just wants to be in touch with his aunt."

"Good Lord, Amy, where'd you pick up all the witchcraft?"

"A friend of mine at UCLA was a spiritualist-medium. He was also a cracking good psychiatrist. He doesn't doubt that some forms of mental illness are caused by demons, and neither do I."

"Run across any demons lately?"

Amy gestured lightly toward the campus. "About one hundred thirty of them."

"Otherwise."

"I've never met any demons, I'm happy to say, and I've never seen a ghost. But I've *heard* plenty of spirits speaking their minds at séances." Craig had his scoffing look again, and Amy smoothed hair over one ear with the palm of her hand. "Now you have another theory of the telephone calls, and I believe my theory might be worth following up."

"Do you feel like a drive?"

"Sure. You mean you *are* taking me seriously?"

"I'm greatly interested."

"That's something," Amy murmured.

"In getting away for an hour with my girl," Craig said, grinning.

Once they were in his Chevelle and on the road to town—a narrow rumpled band of blacktop through heavy woods which Craig called "blind alley"—he had a couple more questions about Amy's preoccupation.

"If it is Michael's ghost, where has he been for sixteen years?"

"Can't tell you, because I don't know that much about the spirit world."

20

"Could he have been right here, in The Shades?"

"You'd like for me to say that's farfetched, but there are well-documented cases of spirits remaining quite near the place where the physical body died."

"So he could be around, but, being a spirit, he's invisible."

"Not necessarily. If he came into the presence of a psychic-sensitive, that person would know immediately. He might even be able to see the spirit as plainly as I see you now."

"Do you know any medium?"

"Not locally. Why?"

"Just curiosity. I've never been to a séance."

She grinned. "An honest medium might make a believer of you in a hurry."

"Don't bet on it. Where are we going; do you have your druthers?"

"Why don't we drive up Big Enoch to the Military Park?"

After the freeze of the night before, the afternoon had a pleasant warmth and the sky was a clear, almost iridescent blue. Craig drove with the top down and after they passed through the village he doubled his speed. Craig was saying something to her but Amy couldn't hear, and she waved for him to slow down.

"We used to live near here," he shouted. "Up that ridge. House is still mostly standing. Want to have a look?"

Craig never had had much to say concerning his boyhood; the talk at lunch about Michael and Michael's fate had greatly increased Amy's curiosity about the unhappy and tragic Young family. She was pleased but a little surprised that Craig was opening up this way, volunteering at last to share what had been a very private part of his life.

Amy nodded, and he slowed almost to a stop before turning at a point where a runneled gravel road came down to meet the county hard road. There were three mailboxes beside the blacktop and as they went by Amy glanced at them. The last of the mailboxes was virtually rusted out but there was a hint of a name still visible on the uphill, weather-protected side of the box. YOUNG.

"Don't know who lives there," Craig said, pointing out an unpainted board house as they went by. "Summer people, I suppose. And the Crofutts live down at the end of that road, or they did the last time I was up this way."

"When was that?"

"I don't know," he replied, looking inexplicably glum. "Months, or years."

"Beautiful," she murmured. "What a wonderful place to live."

"I always thought so." Craig got out of the car, slipped his sunglasses into his shirt pocket and walked toward the abandoned cottage. Halfway there he turned his head quizzically. "You coming? Not much to look at, actually."

She joined him and they stood in front of the east-facing cottage. The roof was half gone, and so was part of one wall; blackened stones were scattered over a large area. Dried moss was thick everywhere, even on the exposed timbers. There were black shards of glass in a few windows. A tall oak which had partly burned along with the cottage still hung protectively, but in a crippled way, over the remains.

Amy stared at the cottage until a squirrel scampered fatly along the roof line. Then she looked up at Craig, who had not taken his eyes from her face.

"As you can see, it burned," he said.

"What happened?"

"Mother. She wasn't the most competent person under ordinary circumstances, but when she drank she was a disaster. We only had the fireplace for heat up here—enough on even the worst winter nights, you understand. But fires need tending, and Mother had the habit of heaping too much wood on the embers and then falling asleep on the sofa. The night the house burned some sparks popped out on the floor. It was lucky she woke up at all, but she did, and got us out through the back door. There's nothing to show you inside; it's just a shell. Melting snow from the roof put the fire out, or I'm sure there wouldn't be a trace of the house today."

Amy looked toward the other side of the clearing and saw a certain amount of litter: paper and tin cans. "Looks like a popular picnic spot. Who owns the property now, Craig?"

"I do. I inherited it at twenty-one."

Amy walked closer to the house. "This is where Michael said he was when he called your aunt late last night. I wonder—"

"For God's sake, Amy," he said dourly. "Let's go. I don't want to hear any more about ghosts."

Amy caught up with him before he reached the car. "I was being thoughtless," she apologized. "I know you didn't have a very happy time in this place."

He looked steadily at her, his eyes expressionless. "You're wrong, Amy. Michael and I were happy. Very happy, I'd say." He leaned back against the Chevelle and took out his pipe, gazing at The Shades through Clark's Gap. "We more or less ran wild in the woods, and we got along fine with Mother—treated her like an older sister. I know a lot more about her today than I did then, of course, and I can see her faults. She drank, and she . . . had no judgment when it came to men, and she neglected us half the time, but we didn't consider her absences neglect. We always knew if she wasn't here one day she'd be here the next, cooking, washing our clothes, trying to get us to wash, taking a fond interest in whatever we happened to be interested in. Seems to me even now that she was very happy, too, although I know better."

"She sounds as if she was a lovely person in spite of her weaknesses."

Amy moved closer to him, and rested her head against his shoulder.

"What happened to your mother, Craig ?"

"After the house burned, Helen decided that Mother was a danger to herself and to us, so—well, she tried to persuade my mother voluntarily to enter Kempton Sanitarium for treatment. But Mother was deathly afraid of places like that. It was necessary to commit her. She died just a few hours after being admitted to Kempton, died of a collapsed blood vessel in her brain while struggling to escape. She was twenty-nine years old."

"That's dreadful."

"She was one of the doomed people we run into from time to time in our work. You feel in your bones as soon as you set eyes on them that they're going to die very young. I suppose Michael had that look, although I can't remember so very much about him. He was Mother all over again: dark, intense, filled with energy, wild and moody." Craig chuckled unexpectedly. "I don't know who I look like, unless there was an uncle Pastiche on the family tree somewhere."

"*I* like the way you look," Amy said, nestling, eyes closed. "Don't go knocking my guy."

Craig put his arm around her. "Meet any interesting men in California ?"

"Dozens."

23

"Are they in love with you?"

"They were when I left."

"Shouldn't have left," he said, shaking his head.

Amy backed off, looking darkly at him and said, "Sometimes I'm not sure when you're joking and when you're not."

"Oh, I'm joking."

"Do you wish I hadn't come back?"

"Don't be silly, Amy."

"I've been waiting all day for a welcome-home kiss, and I still haven't gotten one."

He made a move toward her, sheepishly; she walked back two more steps and said, her eyes still dark and a little hurt, "Too late when I have to ask."

Craig didn't seem to know what to do or say.

"Craig, are we going to get married?"

"I hope so."

"That's something. When?"

"When do you want to get married?"

"When do *you* want to?"

"Tonight," he said.

"No, you don't."

"What are we doing?" Craig said, blinking at her, amiable and perplexed. "We'll both get winded running around in circles like this."

"We've known each other a year and a half," Amy said deliberately. "And I've known that I love you for almost a year now. Six months ago I was sure you were in love with me. Today I'm not sure at all, and I wonder what happened. Don't I wear well? Am I using the wrong bleach? Have I lost my figure?"

Craig smiled meaninglessly.

"Well, *what?*"

"Amy, I love you very much."

"Either, you're lying to me, or else you're taking me for granted."

"I don't think so."

"Maybe," she said angrily, "I've been making too many overnight trips up Ben Lomond Mountain. Is that the trouble, Craig?"

"You know damned well . . . there's no trouble, Amy. I want you as much as I ever have."

She hung her head. "You say it. But I don't feel it."

"I guess . . . we should be getting more definite about marriage."

"Too late when I have to remind you!"

He grinned. "Oh, no, it's not."

Amy poised to run. "Don't think you're going to grab me and—"

Craig lunged at her, and she ran for the nearest tree. He let her think she was going to reach it, then caught up in two strides and pinned her, struggling, against the trunk. Amy kneed his thigh with a ferocious expression but managed not to hurt him. Craig held her easily with one hand and stroked her with the other.

"You've got beautiful eyes," he said gravely. "Should be in pictures."

"I was."

"Prove it."

"Second lead in *Hollywood Blood Beasts!*"

"Believe I saw that one," Craig said. "About fifty times." He kissed her cold cheeks and then, with all the feeling she claimed to have missed, kissed her mouth. Amy was pleased to drop the pretense of a struggle.

After a while they went arm in arm back to the car, both of them flushed. Her hair had bark in it.

"Ben Lomond, here we come," Amy said dreamily.

"Well . . . later, I'm afraid. I'm going to be tied up at the school until around nine."

"Later it is," she vowed.

Amy had her hair combed out by the time they reached the bottom of the ridge, and they were both in high spirits during the drive back. Amy had forgotten completely about Michael Young, the telephone calls and the ruined cottage when Craig said abruptly:

"He must have been on the ridge having a picnic with his family, and heard the story from them."

"Who?"

"The boy who was calling Helen. That's the obvious place for him to have become intrigued by the saga of the Youngs. Well, it's over now. He's through calling." Craig's jaw was set. "He'd better be."

"For Helen's sake I certainly hope so. She didn't have an easy time trying to raise you two, did she?"

"I don't think I gave her much trouble. But Michael wouldn't

25

have anything to do with Helen. I guess he thought she was responsible for our mother's death, and I couldn't make him change his mind. He kept running away, and I'd go after him, and somehow I always found him before he got too far. He put up some terrific fights, but even though I was only about a year and a half older I was a lot bigger, so I'd bring him back. Then one night, I'd say about ten months after Mother died, he ran off right into the teeth of one of the worst blizzards ever to hit down here, and that night I never had a chance. He wasn't found until early spring, deep in a hollow about five miles from here. He was just bones in a creek bed. And that was that. I went away to school the next fall; only made it back to The Shades during the summers and at Christmas. Probably just as well. I might have brooded about Mike otherwise."

"You did everything possible to help him."

"Did I?" He smiled, or grimaced. "Well, I wasn't very old either, and I didn't know how to handle Michael when he was in a fit of despondency. We were close, for brothers, but he just shut me out those times; shut me out."

"You have that tendency yourself, you know."

"What?"

"To shut people out. And when that happens to me, I don't know how to handle it. I get panicky."

"I'm sorry, Amy. Tonight will be different."

"Yes," she said. "I'm counting on that."

The brown-and-white pup came bounding up out of a ditch beside the road and Helen had to twist the steering wheel sharply to avoid running over him. Her ranch wagon veered to the far side of the road before she could bring it under control again. Elsa Britton pushed herself off the dashboard with a gasp.

"Oh, Elsa, I'm so sorry. Are you hurt?"

"Nah, nah, no damage." She shot a look at her friend. "Your face is whiter than that sweater. Wasn't such a close one."

"I hate to admit it, but I've got a case of nerves."

Elsa reached over and patted her shoulder. "Don't you worry; Craig knows about cranks and mental cases. You won't hear from that boy again."

"So far I haven't, but I wish I could be sure he won't call."

"It worries you, bring Peg and come on over to the place tonight."

"What worries me . . ." Helen murmured, coming to a stop

in front of her house.

"How's that ?"

"Elsa, first thing Peg wanted to know this morning was, did Michael call ?"

"Naturally."

They got out, and Helen went around to unlock the tailgate so she could lift out the matching pair of Hepplewhite side chairs she had bought earlier in Gladden.

"And she wanted to see a photograph of Michael."

"Do you have one ?" Elsa asked, helping her with the chairs.

"I wasn't sure when she asked, but I thought if I could show Peg a snapshot of him it might get her off the subject, so I rummaged in a couple of old albums and found a school photo of Michael, taken when he was in the fourth grade." Helen leaned on one of the chairs and looked off down the street. The sky was still blue but it was beginning to get dark.

"Was she satisfied ?"

"Elsa, Peg took one look at the photograph and said 'Oh, yes, I've seen him.' "

"Where did she see him ?"

"On the school playground. Remember last week when she stayed after classes for reunion rehearsals, and I was an hour late getting back from Jack Creek ? She was by herself on the playground until dark: I mean, she was alone except for the boy. He came within a few feet of her, Peggy said, but when she turned and saw him he ran for the woods."

Elsa smiled serenely. "She has a good imagination."

"I suppose he could have come from Greenleaf," Helen mused, "but at that time of day surely they have all of their boys accounted for. Elsa, how well do you remember Michael ?"

"I remember him very well." She picked up one of the battered chairs. "I also remember his funeral," she said emphatically.

"I can get those in the house without any trouble," Helen protested. "Andy'll be wondering what's happened to you. Thanks so much for going with me today, Elsa."

"Ah, I enjoyed it," Elsa said. "Please do me one favor and stop thinking about ghosts."

Helen watched until Elsa had driven away in her vintage Plymouth, and then she picked up one of the chairs and lugged it as far as the porch, where she met an anxious Brenda.

"Supper's ready to go, and I called and called that Peg, but she ain't even answered."

"Do you know where she is, Brenda?"

"Sure! Perched in her tree house. Won't answer me though."

"Well, I'll get her in. Go ahead and serve, Brenda."

Helen left the first chair on the porch, hurried back for the other, locked her car and went around the house to the backyard. It was now getting dark enough so that she had to watch her step to keep from twisting an ankle on a hickory nut.

"Peg!" she called as she approached the tree house, and when her daughter didn't answer, wondered if Brenda had been right about her whereabouts.

Then she heard Peggy sob.

Four

THE BRITTONS' FARM, ONE OF THE BEST IN THE SHADES, LAY ON the eastern slope of Blue Eye Knob, some four miles from the village. At one time Andrew Britton had been the only doctor in The Shades. Then the nearest hospital was a difficult forty-three miles away. Now the community had a thirty-bed hospital and three young physicians, in addition to Andrew, who saw patients only one day a week in the clinic which he had founded. Two days he devoted to his farm, but a good manager looked after the dairy herd and kept them solidly in the black.

This left Dr. Britton considerable free time to devote to hunting and fishing and to another hobby, apiculture.

One of the four substantial barns on the property had been converted into a huge apiary, the environment of which was as rigidly controlled as that of the diary barns. For part of the afternoon the doctor had been unloading bales of hay with the help of Harry Randle, the only one of the hired hands who had no fears about stepping inside the barn, which at times contained upward of a half million bees.

For his age the doctor was a strong and finely conditioned

man and he enjoyed the work, but it was past dark by the time they had completely unloaded the truck and placed the bales against the steel sides of the barn, where they would serve as insulation through the winter.

"Leave the truck by Sam's house when you go down the hill. Getting real foggy out, isn't it?" Ground mist was quite common four out of five autumn nights in The Shades: the roof of his house fifty yards away seemed to be floating on the heavy motionless mist, with the lighted windows looking like pale indistinct flares.

Once Harry Randle was gone Britton went back inside the barn, shutting the steel door after him. The lights overhead were powerful and placed to eliminate shadows. They remained on twenty-four hours a day. He walked slowly across the tan-bark-covered floor to a series of tables which contained positioning hives painted blue, yellow, black and white, the colors bees found most easy to distinguish. On other tables there were feeding stations, painted and unpainted.

A few scout bees were hovering around the empty dishes; as Britton smiled, one of them took off and flew across the barn to the occupied hives a hundred feet away. When he turned back to the tables he felt something unusual and unpleasant: a gust of cold air.

There was a second door in the back wall of the barn and from where he stood the doctor could see that it was standing open a few inches. He scowled; that door was almost always locked, from the inside, and he used it seldom. He walked quickly to the door, opened it wide and looked out.

Behind the barn was a slope of about thirty feet, a few young trees and the new road that twisted up Blue Eye.

The road was invisible in the mist, and the trees were vague presences.

Most of the regular hands on the farm, not liking bees, stayed out of the barn unless they had excellent reasons for being there. Britton wondered who had come in during the day and found it necessary to unlock the back door . . . or perhaps the door had been unlocked for days, and he had never thought to check it. At any rate there seemed to be no point in tracking down the negligent hand, although if the door had blown wide open on a cold night it might have meant trouble for some of his bees. He was mildly angry as he set the lock.

The wall-mounted telephone in his workroom was ringing as

he opened the wooden door at one end. Dr. Britton picked up the receiver.

"Andy? I just got home, so I'm afraid supper won't be until six-thirty at the earliest."

"That's all right; give me time to mark some bees. How was Helen?"

"Still acting snakebit."

"That's too bad. More calls?"

"No. I expect that's over with, and she'll be all right in a couple of days."

"I hope so. Well, ring me when you're ready."

After talking to Elsa the doctor settled down to work. From an open shelf containing many similar bottles and jars he selected an amber bottle with a spray attachment, labeled chloroform. Then he opened several small cans of paint and laid out his delicately tipped brushes on the worktable. "Marking" or numbering bees so that individuals could be traced in a swarm was a fairly simple if tedious job. First the entire colony was put to sleep so the necessary bees could be selected. Then, using an elementary color code—red for 1, yellow for 2, and so on—the doctor could number up to six hundred bees with just five colors, dabbing the shellac-base paint on the thorax or abdomen of each bee. The paint would stay bright and wear for weeks, and from the windows of his prefab building he could observe their flights to and from the hive as he changed the locations of feeding dishes and secondary hives from day to day.

He tied a white gauze surgeon's mask over his mouth and nose, slid back the lid of the hive, picked up a magnifying glass in one hand and the bottle of chloroform in the other and began carefully to spray the inside of the hive.

He did not see the first bee that escaped and stung him, but he wasn't unduly disturbed—sometimes an individual bee wasn't immediately affected by the anesthetic and flew blindly to the light, and it was a mild sting, scarcely more than a pinprick. Despite the mask, he had been holding his breath, so he stepped back for a few moments to give the chloroform a chance to penetrate the cells of the comb. Then he reached out to slide the lid open a little more.

A great gout of black bees seemed to leap from the interior of the hive to fasten on his uncovered hand and wrist, and a numbing shock hit him immediately. He jerked his hand back and the hive toppled from the table, cracking open, the lid falling off.

In agony he brushed at the clot of bees on his hand, scattering a score of them. But already hundreds more were rising from the damaged hive. He stared in disbelief, first at the bees, then at the bottle of chloroform in his hand. He pulled the mask from his face and smelled, not chloroform, but the odor—the stench—of ripe bananas.

With a cry of terror the doctor turned and started for the door, but the unexpected banana scent clung to him, and the bees were all around him, as they would swarm around any intruder threatening their hive.

By the time he reached for the door he could no longer feel the individual stings on his neck and head: it was as if he had been seared by a blowtorch.

Then they were at his eyes.

Dr. Britton was screaming as he smashed into the door and fell to the tanbark outside. He was a beeman and he knew he was going to die, but horror and a mighty instinct for survival kept him going. He rolled and fought the bees, but there were too many of them. Each time he struggled to his feet they drove him down again. He had aroused them and they were furious. They had blinded him, and deafened him. They were wedged in his nostrils and in his open mouth. They covered him like a hideous mask, like a living shirt.

He fell again, and was still.

Elsa was about to put the steaks under the broiler when the telephone in her kitchen rang.

She wiped her hands on her apron and picked up the receiver.

"Elsa? This is Helen. I don't know if I should have called you about this, but Peg was so upset—"

"Something happen to Peggy?" Elsa said sharply.

"No, no, she's all right. But . . . Elsa, there was another call. From Michael. It came while we were on the way home from Gladden. I don't know where Brenda was—in the cellar, I suppose—and Peg answered."

"She talk to him? You sound—"

"Yes, she talked to him. Elsa, where's Andy?"

"With his bees. Why?"

"Michael told Peggy that . . . bad things are going to happen in The Shades, to friends of ours."

"Ha?" Elsa said, forgetting the steaks.

"And that's why I asked about Andy. Michael said . . . he said that Andy—"

Helen didn't have a chance to finish. Elsa dropped the receiver of the wall telephone and hurried across her kitchen to peer out the window over the sink. She could see the lights of the apiary barn through the thickened fog, but little of the building itself. For a few moments she stared in dismay, then returned to the telephone.

"Hang up now, I'll call you back," she said brusquely to Helen.

"Is something—"

Elsa cut her off, then quickly dialed the three digits that would ring the telephone in the barn workroom. The ringing went on for half a minute. When no one answered Elsa replaced the receiver, half ran to the back door, knocking over a chair that was in her way.

"Andy!" she cried.

It was not far across the lot to the barn, but the ground sloped and fog obscured her path. Twice she almost fell, and her heart felt as if it were being pulled apart. She was afraid of another coronary but she was more afraid of this last, ominous phone call from Michael. She wanted to see her husband, and she didn't care how much of a fool she would look when she burst in on him.

"Andy?"

The metal door resisted her the first time she tried to open it. Sobbing for breath, Elsa kicked at it, and stepped inside.

In the shadowless mild air she was confronted by a nightmare of swarming bees.

Beside the door, hanging on the wall, was a beekeeper's veil, heavy protective gloves, a full-length coat of heavy denim and a red cylinder like a fire extinguisher which contained insecticide. After several shocking seconds during which she thought her heart must surely fail, Elsa fumbled for the veil, put on the protective clothing and opened the valve of the tank of insecticide.

I will die, she thought, and found herself praying to die, because he hadn't moved.

Poisoned bees leaped up from the tanbark, stinging futilely at her horseman's boots as she walked deeper into the barn. Bees fell like rain against the impenetrable veil, glanced off the denim coat.

He's strong, she thought. *He may survive this* . . . She saw his face, and gave up hope.

Elsa stood over her husband spraying in every direction, until the noxious fog inside the barn was nearly as heavy as the fog outside, until the furious bees were dead, or had retreated. Then she dropped the red cylinder, knelt clumsily, picked her husband up and carried him in her arms to the nearest door. She was forced to put him down long enough to snap the dead bolt back, and when she tried to pick him up again she found her strength was almost gone. So she grasped Andy under the arms and dragged him outside, into the cold air and the cold fog.

Elsa turned, and caught a glimpse of someone standing close. *Help*, she said, or thought she said. *Help me.*

And then she saw him more clearly, as if the fog had suddenly dissolved where he stood, silently, looking on, his young round fair face expressionless, his dark eyes sad and inquiring. He seemed to have an air of abandonment about him; he had always looked that way to Elsa.

"Michael!" She screamed, and toppled down beside her husband in a faint.

Five

ARON LANDERS' COUSIN CHUCK WAS OVER FROM ROUND SPRING for the day and, although it was early, he was already making Aron's life miserable, as only Chuck knew how. Chuck was nine, barely two years older than Aron, but he was tall for his age and had the kind of insolence which uncritical children accept as sophistication.

It looked like a day impossible to survive without some sort of personal disgrace (he still cried too easily when provoked, the ultimate disgrace with two younger girls looking on) when the possibility of salvation appeared: a fuming, grimy-red motor scooter came chugging down the road at a dead-game twenty miles an hour, carrying a bespectacled man so tall that his knees were nearly at the level of the handle bars as he rode.

"Doremus!" Aron shouted gleefully, and went running toward the oncoming scooter, passing and ignoring Chuck, who was trying to bring the bicycle to a stop with the front wheel in the air.

His motor scooter shuddered pathetically as Doremus Brightlaw slowed and said loudly over the racket of the engine, "Aron; how are you this morning?"

Aron said, panting, "My dad's downtown, Doremus. He'll run me home if I can ride along with you." He'd seen a few of the older kids hitch rides with Doremus, but he was appalled by his own temerity.

Doremus came to a full stop and frowned as he struggled to keep the engine alive. Then he sneaked a casual glance at Aron. Doremus Brightlaw was in his forties; he had a slightly emaciated look, was comfortably weathered and a little bit gray. When he took off his sunglasses to blow the dust of the road from the lenses, his eyes were a light shade of blue and markedly judicial. He took in Aron and Chuck without appearing to and said, "I was about to ask if you'd like to ride along, Aron. Hop on back there."

When Aron was firmly in place, Doremus drove on. The girls ran along beside the road. Doremus waved but Aron was too thrilled to do anything except cling to Doremus' windbreaker.

"Your cousin looks like he's OK," Doremus yelled as they puttered into the village at fifteen miles an hour.

"Yeah, he's OK," Aron allowed, from the heights of his triumph. He saw a couple of kids he knew in front of Rockwell's Café, but he pretended he didn't see them. He was hoping Doremus might be going clear across to the other side of town, but instead Doremus swung into the parking lot behind the post office.

"Where's your dad now?"

"Oh, he's at the MFA. Doremus, if you're going back before lunch..."

Doremus smiled. "No, I'll be a little longer than that, Aron."

"OK." Aron raced off. "I'll see you," he shouted back. "Thanks, Doremus!"

"Come over when you get the time, Aron." Doremus went on into the post office, mailed the once-a-week letter to his sister in Berwyn, Illinois, a suburb of Chicago which he visited dutifully once a year, and then he mailed the once-a-month letter to a man named Vladislav Arshenko, who lived in a suburb of Moscow, a place he'd never laid eyes on and had no desire to visit. Afterward he unloaded his mailbox and went through the accumulated mail leisurely, dropping half of it unopened into the closest wastebasket.

"Might lose out on some big sweepstakes doing that," someone observed.

Doremus glanced up. "Well, you see, it's necessary, Hap. I'm probably one of the world's luckiest men. I mean money's just always stuck to my fingers somehow, and I'm afraid I'd get to winning so many of these things the Treasury Department would set up a branch office in my spare bedroom."

Hap Washbrook leaned against the bank of mailboxes, thumbs hooked over the wide leather belt he wore; because of his girth and the tilt of his Stetson hat, he looked to be a caricature of a county sheriff, all gimme and graft; his bashed and sun-reddened face reinforced the impression. But he was neither dishonest nor a dummy. He'd been a colonel in the Military Police until his retirement from the Army, and his county was annually visited by over a quarter of a million people, including a preponderance of hunters, who brought a lot of guns with them and frequently shot each other, sometimes out of malice. In twenty years Hap had become expert at sorting out the accidental deaths from the suspicious ones, and he knew as much about gunshot wounds as a good medical examiner.

"Now," Hap said thoughtfully, "if I was lucky and won a Cadillac full of cash, I think I'd drive that Caddy down to Acapulco, Mexico. All week I've been thinking about Mexico. You know anything about Acapulco?"

"Not a thing, Hap."

"It's my idea of paradise. Lots of sun, gorgeous women. Of course, I always get like this a few weeks before the deer hunters come in. Give me any other place on earth but Shades County during deer season. Buy you a cup of coffee?"

Doremus agreed and the two men left the post office, walked leisurely down the sidewalk toward the center of the village, past the Little Theater and Weldon's Antiques and the Village Center Art Gallery.

"Haven't seen you around the village last couple of weeks," said Hap. "Occurred to me you might have had some second

35

thoughts about settling down around here."

"Hap, I've been in The Shades two years now, and I look on that as being settled."

"Well, I figured you had a change of heart and threw in with that detective agency's been after you."

Doremus smiled slightly and said nothing.

"Biggest detective agency in the Middle West," Hap mused, pushing open the front door of the Hartshorn Pharmacy. "Wouldn't mind a deal like that for myself."

"They'd make you wear a tie to work, Hap. Besides, it's dull. Like selling shoes."

"This morning I wish I *was* selling shoes."

They sat down in a booth and Hap signaled a waitress. Doremus glanced a second time at the sheriff's reddened weary eyes and said, "Got yourself a bad one, Hap?"

"Andy Britton died last night. Know him?"

"The doctor? He treated me for frostbite last winter. What happened?"

"Some of his bees stung him to death."

"Honeybees?"

Hap gave Doremus a vexed look. "Didn't know there was any other kind. Anyway, he had about half a million of the bastards in his barn, and they jumped him."

"Just like that?"

"I suppose he got careless handling them." The waitress came with their coffee. "One of those jelly doughnuts too, Dolores," Hap said.

"Had he worked around bees long?"

"Elsa told me Andy'd kept bees as long as she can remember, and they were married thirty-eight years. She's the one found him, and she's got a heart condition. Last night it was touch and go, believe me, but I think Elsa will be all right. Tough old German." He looked down glumly at his steaming coffee. "Andy being dead is right hard to take. I admired him, but there's more to it than that. Mind listening?"

"Not at all, Hap."

The sheriff explained in a rambling way about the telephone calls Helen Connelly had received from the boy who called himself Michael, sketched the family history of the Youngs and concluded with the glimpse Elsa had had of "Michael himself."

When he was finished Doremus smoked a miniature cigar halfway before saying, "Are you satisfied that bee venom

36

caused Britton's death ?"

"From the looks of him I'd be real surprised if it was anything else, but the body's going up to Jeff this afternoon for an autopsy. More coffee ?"

"No thanks, Hap. That boy Mrs. Britton saw: could he have been a neighbor ?"

"She didn't know him. I mean he wasn't anybody *living;* he was Michael Young as far as Elsa's concerned."

"And the boy who talked to Helen Connelly's daughter predicted Britton's death ?"

"I haven't been able to get that straight," Hap admitted. "I went over to Helen Connelly's early this morning to find out what Peggy remembered about the phone call, but she's so upset over Andy she won't talk to anybody. Andy more or less took the place of a father, since she never knew her own father."

"Mrs. Connelly a widow ?"

"Her husband was Ed Connelly. Good friend of mine. He was a game warden. Died one spring during a flash flood on the Black Fork. I was wondering, Doremus . . . I really would like to know about the conversation Peggy had with this boy. You've got a knack with the kids which I don't have. If you could spare the time . . ."

"I've been out of police work awhile, Hap."

"I know. But this ain't exactly police work."

"Well . . . I'll be glad to help you out if I can, Hap. But this little girl—Peggy ?—might not want to talk to me either."

They drove in Hap's unmarked car to the Connellys'; Helen was still at the Britton farm, but Craig and Amy met them on the front porch.

"Doremus used to be with the Chicago police," Hap said after introducing him.

Craig looked a great deal more interested than he had upon shaking hands with Doremus. "Oh, really ? What department ?"

"I was a detective."

"Homicide," Hap added.

Craig smiled in a complimentary way. "What brings you to The Shades, Mr. Brightlaw ? Vacationing ?"

"No, I've lived here a couple of years now. Down by Harmony Lake."

"Doremus and I was having some coffee this morning and

I told him about Andy Britton's death—"

Amy said, "Do you still think it was an accident, Sheriff?"

"I have to think so, until something happens to change my mind, Amy."

"I should think"—Amy met Doremus' blandly inquiring eyes and looked down—"I should think you'd be interested in what Elsa saw last night."

"I'm interested in that boy, but I don't have a clue as to who he might be. I'm also interested in the phone calls, which is why I brought Doremus along. He might be able to talk to Peg."

"Well, I doubt it," Craig told the sheriff. "I've been trying all morning to coax her down from that tree house."

"Tree house," Doremus repeated. "Where is it?"

"Out in the backyard, in the tulip tree next to the garage. I'll show you—"

"Oh, I'll find it," Doremus said, and sauntered off, hands in the pockets of his windbreaker.

Doremus reached the tulip tree and walked leisurely around the trunk, looking up at the tree house; leaves crackled under his feet.

"Hey!" he said, after a while, then took off his sunglasses, wiped the lenses on his flannel shirt and listened. He searched his pockets for a stick of cinnamon gum, unwrapped it, chewed thoughtfully and studied the ladder nailed to the tree. Then he began to climb, carefully, the rungs of the ladder creaking under him.

The entrance to the tree house was child-sized, barely wide enough for Doremus to squeeze his shoulders through. He stopped climbing and put his weight on his elbows and looked around, seeing Peggy sitting in one sunlit corner with hostility in her eyes. He paid almost no attention to her but continued to admire the tree house.

"This is all right," he said, squinting. "A little small. When I build my tree house I'll want the roof higher. Ought to be enough room for my dog, too. He spends so much time in trees I think he should have a roof over his head. What do you think?"

Peggy was silent for half a minute, and then she said in a neutral voice, "Dogs can't climb trees."

"Some dogs can't climb some trees."

Peggy considered this, and then explained the absence of a

dog in her tree house by saying, "My dog was run over."

"I'm sorry to hear that."

Peggy looked out the window beside her head. "He wasn't a good dog," she said, with a heavy heart. "He bit."

"Dogs don't always mean to bite."

"He bit though. Does your dog bite?"

"He's too old."

"I've got . . . an old cat."

"I never had a cat."

"And she's . . . a bad cat. She scratches."

"Cats don't always mean to scratch," Doremus said, "Bees don't always mean to sting either."

"Yes . . . they do," Peggy said, tears running down her cheeks. "I hate bees!"

"Sometimes, Peggy—once in a great while—men who work around bees, like the doctor, get stung, and sometimes they die. Nobody knows for sure why it happens."

Peggy sobbed. "Michael made it happen!" She wanted to go ahead and cry, but the presence of Doremus inhibited her, so she wiped furiously at her eyes, her mouth a thin white line.

"Did he tell you he'd make it happen, Peggy? Did he say the bees were going to sting Dr. Britton?"

"He said . . . bad things were going to happen. He said A-Andy was going to . . . get hurt. It's Michael's fault, he did it! I hate Michael!"

"Do you know him very well?" Doremus asked calmly, not pressing Peggy but giving her enough to think about to keep her from turning away into a brooding silence.

"No."

"I know a boy named Michael Landers—Aron's big brother. Do you know Mike?"

"Yes. He's twelve."

"That's right, he is. But that wasn't who you talked to yesterday."

"No. It was Michael Young."

"Did he tell you that himself?"

"He said . . . his name was Michael, and he said he talked to my mother. I knew who he was."

"But you never talked to him before."

"I saw him once. On the playground. He ran away."

"He didn't talk to you then?" asked Doremus.

"He just . . . ran away."

"I'd like to see him sometime myself," Doremus said. "Would you tell him that if you talk to him again?"

"I don't . . . *ever* want to talk to him again," Peggy said, shaking her head.

"He's just a little boy, Peggy. And he can't hurt anybody, not really. And maybe he didn't mean to scare you. It's not much fun when you're all by yourself."

"Is he all by himself?"

"Whoever he is, I think he's awfully lonely."

"Do you think he's dead?"

"No, I don't, Peggy."

Peggy was affected by his certainty. "Mother showed me his picture," she said, but she seemed tired of the subject of Michael. Her eyes were dry again. "Are you going to build a tree house?" she asked Doremus.

"I've been seriously thinking about it."

"Where do you live?"

"At Harmony Lake. Know where that is?"

Peggy nodded. "Craig and Amy took me swimming there this summer."

"You probably saw my house. My name's Doremus. Do-re-mus."

"Do-re-mus," Peggy pronounced, meticulously.

"Would your mother give me a drink of water if I ask her?"

"Yes. But she might not be here. She went to—"

"That's OK, I'll just help myself if you won't show me."

"Oh, I'll show you," Peggy said promptly. She got up and came over to the opening in the floor of the tree house. "You have to be careful going down," she cautioned. "I fell once. Mother wouldn't let me come up here for a week."

When they were both on the ground they walked together to the back porch. "There's Mother," Peggy said delightedly, breaking into a run, and Helen Connelly came outside, wearing a neat black wool dress, unadorned.

"He wants a drink of water," Peggy said.

"Good morning, Mrs. Connelly. I'm Doremus Brightlaw."

"How do you do, Mr. Brightlaw. Would you like to come in? The others are in the kitchen."

After Peggy had had a glass of milk, Helen coaxed her upstairs to take a bath and returned to find Doremus discussing the meaning of the "Michael" telephone calls with Craig.

Doremus said, "Mrs. Britton saw a young boy resembling

the Micheal Young she knew, and Peggy saw a boy she believes is Michael. But both of these occurrences might be unrelated to the calls, which in turn are not necessarily related to the death of Dr. Britton."

"How can you say that?" Amy responded indignantly. "Yesterday that boy as much as promised Andy would be killed, and less than an hour later he turns up at the barn where Andy has been stung to death by bees!"

"So far," Hap said, "there's only Elsa's testimony that a boy was there, and she was—well, she was almost hysterical; no telling what she actually saw. Probably some kid taking a shortcut home through the barn lot."

"I believe Elsa," Amy said more quietly. "It may have been an apparition, but she saw Michael."

Craig shook his head wearily. "Ghosts again."

Helen held out a small photograph to Doremus. "I thought you might be interested in seeing this, Mr. Brightlaw. It's a school picture of Michael Young, taken just a couple of months before he died."

Doremus accepted the photo and studied it closely, then passed it on to Hap. Amy and Craig looked over his shoulder.

Craig's expression was bleak. Amy glanced at him sympathetically, seeming a little sorry for her talk about apparitions.

"He looks a lot like the middle Boyer kid," Hap murmured. "A little thinner, maybe."

Hap rose from the kitchen table. "Helen, I'd like to keep this picture for a while if you don't mind. Show it around."

"Will Elsa have to see it?" Amy asked.

"I'm afraid so."

"Oh, Hap," Helen said glumly.

"Doremus, care to ride along with me to the Britton place?" Hap said, and Doremus surprised him by assenting.

When they were in the sheriff's car and on the way to the Britton farm, Hap said to Doremus, "That's a mighty lot of woman back there."

"Like to hear about her sometime," Doremus said pleasantly as he smoked his cigar, but he was staring out the window and he seemed to be somewhat bored. He had nothing more to say until they reached the farm. There Hap pointed out the barn in which Dr. Britton had been stung to death, and Doremus perked up.

"OK if I poke around inside, Hap ?"

"Sure, the barn's not padlocked. Need to spend a few minutes with old Elsa. There's still plenty of bees inside, so watch yourself."

"Tell me one thing, Hap. Where was the doctor when the bees attacked him ?"

"Inside his workroom. You'll see it."

Doremus nodded, got out of the car and headed for the barn, pausing to stomp out his cigar on the way.

For more than a minute after entering, he stood by the door studying the layout of the apiary, and then he proceeded slowly across the tanbark in the artificial brightness to the place, marked with stakes and string, where Andrew Britton had fallen. He looked at the discarded insecticide tank, then took a pocket knife from his trousers and, hunkered down, began prying carefully with the blade in the packed-down tanbark. He exhumed one of the dead bees, held it up on the blade to the level of his eyes and squinted at it. With his other hand he reached into his shirt pocket, slipped the cellophane off the package of cigars he carried there and dropped the bee into this makeshift bag. With the bee stowed away, he went all around the staked area, occasionally squatting to pick up more bees with the knife.

He made a survey of the bottles and jars on the shelves over the worktable, then noted the jars of paint on the table itself, and what looked like a discarded surgeon's mask. That brought a frown. For several minutes he was motionless, thinking. Finally he squatted down and saw a bottle with a spray attachment that had rolled partway under one section of the shelves. He reached for it and read the label: *Chloroform*.

Automatically he held the bottle close to his nose and sniffed twice.

He was so puzzled by the contradictory odor from the amber "chloroform" bottle that he almost sprayed some of the liquid on his hand, but instinct warned him not to. He turned for another lingering look at the hive on the floor, then rose and placed the bottle on the table.

"Anything wrong with that ?" Doremus was asked.

He looked around quickly. Harry Randle was standing just outside the workroom.

"Found it on the floor," Doremus said amiably. "Who are you ?"

"Randle. I work for the Brittons."

"I didn't see you come in."

Harry jerked his head toward the back door, which was standing open. "You from the State Patrol?"

Doremus only smiled and left the workroom, having decided to go out by way of the back door. Randle followed him leisurely. Outside, the ground was rocky for a distance of about ten feet, then there was a slope covered with frostbitten weed, some bright hawthorn and a couple of Chinese elms growing near the trim white-painted fence beside the road.

"Please don't touch anything inside if you can avoid it."

"Why would I do that? Should I fix the lock on the door when I leave?"

"Might be a good idea." Doremus strolled around the barn to Hap's car. The sheriff had come down from the house and was talking by radio to his office.

"Any problems with the bees?" Hap said, after he'd replaced the radio microphone.

"No." Doremus produced the cellophane sack he'd made. "I borrowed one, if you don't mind."

Hap grimaced. "Take 'em all. Old Elsa's going to have the lot burned anyhow."

"Is she? That's a shame. Looks as if the only German bees the doctor had were the ones that took after him. I suppose these are the U.S. variety of Germans, and not imported. There are a couple of nice colonies of Italian bees in there, and two hives of Caucasians. Both fine breeds, and not excitable. Cyprian bees are probably nastier than the Germans, but they're yellow. I didn't notice any dead yellow bees around the spot where he died."

The sheriff smiled a lopsided, admiring smile. "So you're a bee expert."

"Not at all. My Uncle Swen keeps bees on his farm in Wisconsin, but I've forgot half of what I ever learned from him. Believe I'll give him a call."

"Find out something interesting?" Hap said quickly.

"Can't say that I did, but I'd like to know what would make those German bees swarm so suddenly that an experienced beekeeper would panic. He was just a few feet from the door, and safety, and he'd been bitten before, I'm sure. I think maybe a couple hundred of them stung him at once."

"Even an autopsy couldn't determine that. Is it unusual?"

43

"Damned unusual." Doremus put his dead bee back in a pocket of the windbreaker and stood smoking and gazing at the blue sky. Hap nibbled at a thumbnail.

"This *was* an accident, wasn't it, Doremus?"

Six

DOREMUS OWNED SEVERAL WOODED ACRES AND A SMALL HOUSE built on a mighty slab of limestone overlooking a wide stretch of the spring-fed Competition River; the half-mile-long part of the river was not deep enough to be called a lake but here the often turbulent river slowed and eddied peacefully much of the year, turning a deep green color, and so someone a long time ago had tagged the place Harmony Lake.

Most of Saturday afternoon following his visit to the Britton farm he spent on his hands and knees nailing porch flooring in place, watched over by three railbirds named Tim, Maisy and Seth, who handed down tools or nails when he asked for them and managed to stay out of his way.

The telephone inside the house rang for what seemed like the tenth time that afternoon.

The caller wasn't his Uncle Swen in Wisconsin; it was Helen Connelly.

"Mr. Brightlaw, I'm terribly embarrassed to call, but you were so nice to Peggy this morning that I wonder if—" She lost her voice momentarily, then continued in a rush, "Peg's not there with you, is she?"

"No, I haven't seen her since I left your house, Mrs. Connelly. Is she missing?"

"I'm . . . afraid so. I drove Peg to the Methodist Church early this afternoon with several of the other neighborhood children to rehearse for the reunion—the whole thing was going to be called off, but Elsa heard and said no, Andy wouldn't have wanted it that way. Well, I left the children at the church and went on to Elsa's. I had intended to stay about an hour, but once I got there I felt I just couldn't leave right away, and then when I reached home a little while ago Peggy wasn't here. One of the mothers was supposed to drive her home but there'd been a lot of confusion at the church, of course, with a hundred boys and girls—"

"Peggy doesn't have another hideout, does she?"

"I beg your pardon?"

"Other than the tree house."

"I see what you mean. No, only the tree house. I called everyone I could think of, but Peggy's not visiting any of her usual friends. Then I tried the church, and Reverend Bartlett remembered seeing her with Maisy Duncan, and that's how the whole thing has gotten around to you." Helen laughed, but clearly she was worried. "Peg's not a thoughtless child, and she's not given to wandering off—"

"Let me see what Maisy has to say," Doremus suggested, and called the little girl into the kitchen. "Did you talk to Peggy Connelly today?" he asked her.

Maisy nodded. "At the church."

"Did Peggy ride home with you?"

"No, sir."

"Did your mother bring you home?"

"No, sir."

"Who did?"

"I forget."

"Could you try to remember?"

Maisy made a stab at concentration, her eyes on the ceiling. "Mrs. Cummings."

"Did Peggy tell you where she was going to be this afternoon?" Maisy shook her head. "OK," Doremus said. "There's root beer in the icebox. Would you help yourself and give a couple to the boys?" Doremus repeated what Maisy had told him for Helen's benefit.

"I'll just have to get in the car and go looking. I'm sorry again for—"

"Excuse me, Mrs. Connelly . . . What was that, Maisy?"

Blond Maisy was on tiptoe, reaching into the refrigerator. "Said she was going to look for Michael."

"Peggy said that? Why didn't you tell me before?"

Maisy shrugged and carefully set another bottle of root beer on the floor.

Doremus glanced at his wristwatch. It was five minutes past

four. His hand was covering the speaker of the telephone receiver. "Michael who?" he asked.

"Welllll . . . *I* don't know."

"The opener's right there on the cabinet, Maisy." Doremus looked dubiously at the receiver in his hand and then said to Helen, "Maisy remembers now that Peggy mentioned something about going to look for Michael."

After a two-second hesitation Helen said in a low voice, "Dear God."

"Mrs. Connelly, I'd like to help you look for Peggy, unless you have some other ideas about where she might be."

"I don't, no. Should I call the sheriff?"

Doremus responded to her hint of fear by saying, "I doubt that'll be necessary." He glanced at Maisy, who was prying the caps off the bottles of root beer. "Right now I have company," he told Helen, "and it will be about ten minutes before I can start them home. If you wouldn't mind driving down this way . . ."

"Not at all," Helen said instantly.

"Good. I'm at the end of Competition Road, where it turns to gravel."

By the time Helen Connelly reached Doremus' house the sun was low in the trees, its light clear but remote, and where Doremus stood waiting the porch was dark.

Helen said when they were under way, "I don't understand what would compel Peg to go off on her own—she isn't that adventurous. She must still be very upset with Mi—with whoever-he-is. I explained to her as carefully as I could that Michael Young died many years ago, but of course she talked to 'Michael' on the telephone, so he seems as real as any of the boys she knows." Helen smiled tensely. "He seems real to me."

"Where is the Methodist Church, Mrs. Connelly? Almost in the village, isn't it?"

"Yes, it's at the corner of Scotia and Pine."

"Did Peggy have any money with her?"

"I think she had about twenty cents in her purse."

"Chances are she got as far as the village center, then decided to have a soda. Now she's wondering how to get home."

Helen, who was ready for any agreeable explanation of Peggy's absence, said ruefully, "I must be losing my mother's instinct. That's what she's done. I'll bet she's in Huffaker's right now, talking Charley's ear off. Charley was her summer's

46

love—he's fifteen, and he taught her to swim." Helen slowed for a stop sign. The sky in the east was darkening from rain clouds. "I'm afraid I've wasted quite a lot of your time, Mr. Brightlaw. There's no point in your riding all the way to the village with me if you'd rather—"

"It's no waste of time. And, uh, if you don't mind—uh, Doremus?"

"If I can stop being Mrs. Connelly. If I may say so, you know a great deal about children and their ways, Doremus. Do you have children of your own?"

"No. My sister has quite a brood though. So Marian and I sort of borrowed her kids from time to time."

"You're married then?"

"Was married. Say, do you mind if I smoke a cigar?"

Helen didn't mind, and once Doremus had his cigar going he lost a certain amount of his reserve, or timidity, or whatever it was, and seemed more at home with her.

Helen double-parked in front of Huffaker's sandwich shop and went in, but she was back quickly, shaking her head. "Charley hasn't seen her today. Let's see . . . the variety store is closed, but there are two other places Peg likes to visit.

"I'll call home," Helen said, but she got only Brenda, who reported that Peggy had neither "showed her face" nor called.

When Helen returned to the ranch wagon the sky was two-thirds dark, and Doremus was starting his second cigar. For half a minute Helen sat with her hands on the wheel, not knowing where to go, and then she said, giving up all pretense of good cheer, "This is beginning to scare me. It's ten after five."

"Chances are she's with a friend," Doremus said calmly. "Dinnertime will come before long and Peggy'll remember she has a home. It might be best if you went back to your house, because she's bound to call. You can leave me at the Trailways depot; the six-o'clock bus to Polar Bluff will drop me off five minutes from my place."

"I wouldn't think of doing that," Helen said automatically, staring at the lighted telephone booth she had just left. Her skin looked preternaturally white under the sodium-vapor parking-lot lamp and her curled lip seemed frozen, sickened. She said, with an audible intake of breath, "What I'm afraid of now . . . She wanted to find Michael. Instead he found her. Again. And this time he didn't run away."

47

Doremus turned his head sharply. "Would you tell me that again?"

"When I showed Peggy Michael Young's school photo—the same one I gave to the sheriff—she said, 'Oh, yes, I've seen him.' And when I asked her where—" Helen broke off, looking astonished. "*That's* where she is! She saw this boy she believes is Michael on the school playground two or three weeks ago. As far as Peggy is concerned, that's the place to look for him again."

The Shades consolidated school, located directly under Constable Ridge, was less than half a mile away along the same road they were on. There were asphalt parking lots on both sides of the four-building complex and playing fields behind it. The front of the school and the parking lots were well lighted. Helen made a single sweep around the school, but neither of them saw Peggy. She then stopped behind the cafeteria and Doremus got out, looking across the playing fields to the black rise of the heavily wooded ridge.

"I see somebody," he said. "Honk your horn." Helen leaned on the horn and also rolled down her window and called.

Presently Peggy came running through the gloom and arrived out of breath and red in the face. Helen was both angry and concerned at the sight of her daughter.

"I've been searching for you," she snapped. "All over the place."

"I wanted to see Michael," Peggy explained, in a low voice.

"Peggy—" Helen started ominously, but Doremus cut her off.

"Did you see him?"

Peggy eyed Doremus again, and decided she had an ally. "No. He lives in the woods. But he didn't come out today. I wanted to tell him"—Peggy's mouth turned down and her face looked redder than before—"I wanted to tell him to leave us alone, and not . . . not hurt anybody else. Like he hurt Andy." She lowered her eyes and stood looking miserably at the ground.

"Baby," Helen said, more gently, "please get in the car now."

"I don't want to . . . if you're going to be mad at me."

"I'm not mad anymore. We'll just forget about the whole thing. And we'll forget about Michael too."

After supper Peggy amused Doremus by showing off her

48

favorite antiques while Helen did the dishes. Peggy's favorites numbered in the hundreds and she could talk about them almost as well as her mother could, but Doremus' interest and patience never seemed to waver. Helen didn't know if he cared for antiques, and ordinarily she would have called Peggy off after a few minutes to give him a rest; however, she had a notion that Doremus would have been as disappointed by this as Peggy.

Outside, the rain had begun to come down heavily but peacefully, without wind or thunder. Helen had a second cup of coffee in the kitchen after loading her dishwasher and then went in search of her guest, who was sitting on a horsehair settee in what had been the parlor of the house, cigar smoke curling around his head, while Peggy explained the purpose of a Georgian silver pap dish.

"Doremus has a telephone call to make while you put all those things back," Helen said.

"Then I think I'd better be on my way."

"The telephone's in the hall," Helen explained, as Doremus accompanied her. "But I can move it to my office without any trouble—"

"That isn't necessary. I just want to give my Uncle Swen a ring and ask him a couple of questions about bees."

"Oh," Helen said. "About bees?" She was about to return to the parlor to help Peggy straighten up but Doremus motioned for her to stay.

"Uncle Swen? This is Doremus. . . . Yehp, Doremus. . . . No, I'm not in Chicago, I'm down here in . . . Well, they're all fine far as I know, all seven of 'em. . . . You didn't hear? No, there's seven now; I'm sure they must have sent you an announcement. Karl fell out of a tree this summer and broke his arm . . . That was *last* summer; this time it was his arm, but not his pitching arm. Uncle Swen, what I called about, there was a man down here stung to death by bees yesterday, and . . . German bees, Swen. . . . Yehp, that's exactly the way I'd describe them. . . . No, he knew what he was doing; he'd handled bees for years. This was indoors, and he was using what he thought was chloroform on the colony before he removed some of the bees for experimental purposes. Only I don't think it *was* chloroform; it had a different odor. Like ripe bananas."

Doremus picked up his cigar and clamped it into his mouth,

and he listened without uttering a sound for what seemed like five minutes to Helen, and as he listened, new, hard lines came into his face and he looked like a different man. She couldn't help shuddering as the rain roared down on the roof.

"All right, Swen, thanks for the information. One more thing: what sort of effect would a ghost have on a hive full of bees?" Doremus grinned suddenly and held the receiver of the telephone slightly away from his ear so Helen could hear the hoarse laughter of Uncle Swen in Wisconsin.

When he could get a word in, Doremus said, "Just a little blackberry cordial after supper, Swen. Thanks again for the information; I'll let you know all about it one of these days. . . . No, I'm still retired. Just sort of poking around the edges of what might be a murder case."

He hung up, still grinning, but when he saw Helen's shocked face he looked bleak and sorry for his slip of the tongue.

"How could Andy have been murdered?" Helen asked quietly, looking to see that Peg was nowhere around.

"I'm not sure," Doremus said hastily. "But I have a clear idea now of what happened to him. He thought he was spraying a solution of chloroform into the opened hive, but the contents of the bottle was something else altogether: an essence of bee venom, strong enough to provoke bees into suicidal rage. A honeybee can only sting once, you know, and then it dies, and bees seem to realize this, so nearly all varieties will put up with a heck of a lot before committing themselves to a sting and death. On the other hand, even the best-natured bees will swarm and sting occasionally for mysterious reasons. As far as my Uncle Swen knows, all bees react violently to the odor of venom. A couple of times he's had to burn those elbow-length gloves beekeepers sometimes wear because the gloves have become saturated with bee venom, and to handle a hive while wearing them might bring on an attack."

"Andy must have made a mistake and used the wrong bottle," Helen said.

"That's entirely possible. The bottle was labeled chloroform, but there were many brown and amber bottles on his workroom shelves, some labeled, some not. Undoubtedly one of those contains chloroform. I'll find that out in the morning." Doremus decided his cigar was becoming rank and put it out in a nearby ashtray. "I'm sorry I used the word *murder;* it's unjustified. Conceivably someone who knew a great deal about Dr. Britton's hobby and afternoon schedule, and quite a lot about bees as well, could have switched labels on two bottles of chloroform and bee venom, which would be as effective as putting a shotgun to the doctor's head, and much safer. It's also conceivable that one of the hands on the Britton farm, sent into the workroom for some purpose or other, got panicky or in too much of a hurry because of the nearness of all those bees, knocked several bottles from the shelves and then in confusion mislabeled them. I'd want a chemist or pharmacist to check the contents of every bottle in that workroom, to make sure the contents matched the label. I suppose Hap can have someone do that."

"What if only the venom bottle was mislabeled?"

"Then I'd be inclined to think that it was done on purpose."

Helen looked for a chair, sat down, hands joined in her lap. "By a—by who? And why? Andy Britton was— I can't believe anyone could dislike him enough to cause his death in such a horrible way."

"I'd look for simple motives. A long-held grudge, for instance. How old was the doctor? About sixty-five? Probably that rules out women"—Helen looked offended—"but not inevitably." Doremus put the telephone back on the Sheraton table and walked to the front door, stood gazing out at the planetary street light through a waxen shower of rain. "I'd look for simple motives, but there's the problem of Michael. Who is he, and what does he know? What do *we* know about him? As your nephew Craig says, he's a boy with an amazingly inventive mind, what appears to be an endless capacity for fantasy, and at least a touch of evil. He also has a capacity for getting around—and it's almost too good to be true that Mrs. Britton should happen across him as she's dragging her dead husband from the barn." Doremus pondered his suppositions. "Chances are we're dealing with as many as three boys, all about the same age, linked together by coincidence alone. Or else we're involved with the supernatural, as Miss Lawlor seems to think but that offends good sense and makes any kind of logical detective work impossible."

Doremus turned to look at Helen, and his expression became less severe. "Tell me about Michael Young," he said. "How long was he missing before his body was found?"

"There wasn't . . . a body. Just clothing, and bones. I believe it was seven months altogether before berry-pickers discovered the remains, in a gully where he'd fallen."

"How was he identified ? By dental charts ?"

"No. I recognized the plaid coat he'd had on the night he disappeared. That seemed to be . . . enough."

"He'd be about twenty-six today, wouldn't he ?"

"Yes," Helen said.

"If he were alive," Doremus said—and Helen came halfway up out of her chair—"if Michael Young were alive after all, then some of our questions would be answered. But that possibility offends good sense too—" He caught sight of Helen again and seemed surprised and chagrined by her reaction. "Sorry, I have this habit of thinking out loud. Say, it's almost eight-thirty; you must be ready to throw me out by now."

She wanted very much to be alone and so she protested badly, and Doremus was aware of it; they had nothing to say to each other while Peggy ran upstairs for her own and her mother's coat. Doremus watched the rain come down and retreated into remoteness behind a cigar and Helen simply waited, enduring the wait and the rain and the prospect of a long drive. It was a depressing end for what had been a lively evening.

Seven

THE RAIN HAD STOPPED COMPLETELY BY THE TIME HELEN WAS ON the road back from Doremus' house, with Peggy asleep beside her on the front seat. The air was still and wet and chilly and the moon was trying to come out, but Helen didn't see the black overflow from the little river in the hollow until she rounded a bend and plunged down into it at thirty-five miles an hour.

Wings of water drenched the windshield but she didn't panic and, relying on memory, she kept the ranch wagon on the road until she was out of the hollow and the overflow, at which time she recovered sufficiently from shock to start trembling, knowing that if they had veered off the road into the river itself they probably would have drowned.

At the top of the next rise Helen pulled over and stopped for a few moments to regain her composure, and while she was sitting there the lights flickered and dimmed and she discovered that the engine had died.

She glanced at Peggy, who unaccountably had slept through the explosion of car into water and who continued to sleep blissfully with her hands clasped under one cheek. But it had been a long, trying day for Peggy. Helen sighed and wished they were home and tried to start the engine.

After the fourth try she succeeded in killing the lights altogether. Helen knew nothing about automobiles, but she knew that they needed electricity to run, and that undoubtedly there were wires somewhere which must be soaking wet from the overflowing river. So she and Peggy would go nowhere until a car came by.

In the meantime they were alone in the dark without lights or heat. The moon had broken through high clouds and her surroundings were visible, but Helen didn't need the moon to know exactly where she was, and she was aware of how seldom anyone traveled that particular road after dark. She then began to worry that someone *would* come, from the direction in which she had come but at a higher speed, and have an accident. Hap should know about the overflow, Helen decided, and she felt sure he would send a car for her.

She opened the door and got out, taking care not to disturb Peg. There were three mailboxes a few feet from where she had parked, and a gravel road angled up the ridge above her. It was so quiet she could hear rain dripping from the leaves in the woods.

Three houses on the ridge, Helen thought. But one had burned more than sixteen years ago, and was abandoned; she would not go there. A family named Kutner owned a house about halfway up the road, a distance of perhaps two hundred yards, but Helen could not remember if they were summer people. She told herself that if no one was at home she would not mind breaking in to use the telephone; otherwise she would have to take Peg and walk more than a mile down the dark country road to a point where it intersected Route 22.

Helen turned and looked through the closed window at her sleeping daughter, then decided to lock both doors. Her footsteps sounded unnaturally loud to her as she walked around the ranch wagon to Peg's side and turned the key in the door lock.

It worried her to leave Peggy alone even for ten minutes, but the wagon was pulled well off the blacktop, and probably nothing would happen to disturb her daughter's sleep.

With the doors locked, Helen walked quickly up the rutted and rain-slicked road, finding her way by the moon. The wood lot to her left was filled with a light luminous mist and looked beautiful in a desolate way. On her right was a crowding woods, impenetrable; it was like a reflecting wall, sending back the sounds of her own hurried breathing.

She paused to rest, hoping for a lamp in a window of the Kutner place to guide her the rest of the way, but she couldn't see one.

Instead there was a light like a steady beacon much farther on, at the top of the ridge, where she was certain no one lived.

Without having to think about it, Helen started walking again toward the light. The road was worse, loose gravel and clay, and she slipped twice, the second time going down on one knee. Because she was wearing slacks she wasn't hurt, but as she was getting up she saw him, standing perhaps a hundred feet away in the misty wood lot.

The image of a boy in the wood lot was so compelling—like the inexplicable light above—that at first she felt only a minor current of fear. She strained to distinguish the motionless figure, but the moon was wrapped in a cloud and the figure disappeared gradually, black into black. Her eyes smarted and Helen rubbed at them, and then the fear cut into her strongly, numbing her throat, and she hurried on, not really seeing the road, heedless of falling. Even the light atop the ridge had temporarily vanished, leaving her disoriented and alone. She sobbed for breath, stopped with a jerk, looked back.

Moonlight again spread through the wood lot, but no one was there.

I saw him, she thought. I saw—

She would not let herself think of whom she had seen.

It was too late to turn around and go back. Already she had come three-quarters of the way and the ridge had leveled. The friendly light was shining, bigger than the moon, white and strong, through a gap in the woods. She would find someone there, Helen thought. Someone real, who would help her.

When she was within a few feet of the cottage, directly in front of the dazzling jagged window, she stopped, pinned down by fear. The light now seemed unearthly to her. There was nothing inside, there was no one; how had the light gotten there?

The cracked glass of the window seemed to leap out at her, a thousand dazzling pieces, and the light was gone. In the space of the window a face appeared.

Helen turned away, screaming, and caught a glimpse of him scrambling over the windowsill, coming after her. She tried to run and fell to her knees.

A hand seized her shoulder.

"Good God," Craig Young said. "Helen? What are you doing up here?"

She recoiled from the flashlight beam against her eyes. "Craig?"

"Let me help you up. You scared the wits out of me, Helen."

"I . . . I scared *you!*"

"Are you hurt?"

"No . . . fine. I'm . . . my wagon stalled . . . on the road down there, and . . . I walked up to see if one of the summer houses was . . . occupied. Saw there was a light up here. I didn't want to come but—" She broke off and stared up at her nephew. "Craig? Have you . . . been here long?"

"I'd say about twenty minutes. One of Hap's deputies told me a gang of kids had been up this way, making themselves at home. I wanted to put a stop to it."

"Kids?" Helen repeated. "Craig, I saw a . . . I think it was a young boy . . . in the wood lot down there. Just standing between a couple of trees, watching the road. He couldn't have been more than . . . than ten, and he was alone."

"I'd like to find him. He may be one of the gang who's moved in here."

"Moved in?"

"I'll show you what I mean," Craig said grimly, and led her around the cottage to a space where the back door had been. Helen held back involuntarily but Craig angled the powerful beam of his flashlight inside. "Over there."

Helen stared at an Army-style bed with a mattress against one burned and blistered wall of what had been the kitchen of the house. This area was still roofed over and relatively well protected from snow and rain.

"No telling how long that's been up here," Craig said. "But the metal is rusting and the mattress has mildewed. I suppose that's no difference to the little bastards. They just throw a blanket over the mattress and make out all right."

"Craig, the boy I saw . . . he wasn't old enough for . . ." Helen paused, looking thoughtfully at the bed. "Craig, why did you smash that window ? Didn't you see me ?"

Craig grinned. "I saw somebody coming, and I was in the mood to give them a fright. I'm sorry; no way I could know—"

"Of course not."

"I'm going to throw that bed down the steep side of the ridge," Craig vowed, pointing his light into the depths of the gutted house, "and then one of these days when I've got a little money I'll restore this place. It'll be just the way it was."

Helen said without thinking, "I doubt if Amy—" And then she decided this was presumptuous. "I had to leave Peg in the wagon," she explained, "and I'm afraid she's going to wake up and find me gone. I didn't see your car—"

"Oh, I hid it the other side of the clearing. Are you feeling better now ?"

"Much better."

"What did you say was the matter with your wagon ?"

"Drowned out, I'm afraid. There was an overflow from the river and I didn't see the water in time."

"We'll get it started. If not, you can drive the Chevelle in and send somebody back for me." He shifted the light and they started back to the clearing, picking their way through heaps of stones and across a rotting timber, walking beneath the crippled oak that stood ineffectual guard over the remains of the house that only Craig seemed to care about anymore.

Peggy sat up straight in the front seat of the ranch wagon, aware that they had stopped, aware that it was dark and quiet. Somehow she knew, though she was not fully awake, they had not stopped in front of their house.

She heard someone trying to open the door behind her, and she turned her head, saying, "Mother ?"

Craig braked his Chevelle halfway down the ridge and Helen pointed out the place where—as well as she could remember—she had seen the figure in the woods. Craig flashed his light among the trees, but the light revealed nothing.

"Whoever he is," Helen said, "I hope he has a home to go to. He seemed so lonely standing there, as if . . . he'd been waiting forever."

Craig said sourly, "I thought you didn't get a good look."

"It wasn't what I saw, it was what I felt—Craig!"

They both heard Peggy's voice at the same time, a faint echo to it, as if she were crying from the depths of a well.

"Mother! Mother . . ."

Craig put the car in gear and gunned down the hill, headlights illuminating the tall trees on both sides of the road, pooling suddenly on the blacktop road below.

"There she is!" Helen said. "Stop, Craig, let me out!"

Peggy scrambled toward them, and Helen threw open the door and ran to meet her.

"I saw him, Mother! Michael was here! He came right up to the car!"

Helen hugged her daughter tightly, but Peggy tried to pull away.

"Let's find him, Mother! He was right here!"

"Baby . . ."

Craig came loping toward them. "What's the matter, was she having a nightmare?"

"Uncle Craig, I saw Michael! He looked in the window at me, and then he disappeared!"

"He ran away?" said Craig, looking stunned.

"No, he disappeared! Like a ghost."

"Peggy . . . Peg," Helen said urgently. "Calm down now. Tell me exactly what happened."

Peggy was not about to calm down, but she said more precisely, "I woke up and you weren't there, and then I heard him trying to open the door and I turned around and it was Michael. When I looked at him he disappeared. So I got out of the car, but by then he was gone."

Craig trotted over to the ranch wagon with his flashlight in his hand, studied the gravel below the right-side door, then went on more deliberately along the shoulder of the blacktop, aiming his flashlight here and there. Helen lifted Peggy and carried her toward the wagon.

"He was here, Mother!" the wide-eyed Peggy insisted.

"Yes, yes, I believe you. But he's gone now. Peggy, he's gone and he's not going to come back. So we might as well go home, don't you think?"

"Can we come back in the morning? I want to *see* him."

Helen felt as if she were going to cry. "I don't know . . . maybe he doesn't want us to see him. We'll t-talk about it in the morning."

"Are you all right, Mother? Where was Uncle Craig?"

"The car stalled. I went to find help and fortunately for us he came along."

"I told Michael to wait. I told him I wasn't going to hurt him. I told him! Why did he disappear?"

Craig had come back; Helen glanced at him hopefully but he just shrugged and looked doubtfully at Peggy.

"No footprints . . . except a couple that must be yours, Helen."

"Uncle Craig, what's the matter with Michael? Is he mad at us?"

Craig ignored the question. "Could I have your keys, Helen? I'll see if I can get this thing started."

He unlocked the driver's door and slid in under the wheel of the ranch wagon. Nothing happened when he turned the key in the ignition. Then he got out, lifted the hood, studied the alternator for a few seconds, made an adjustment, slammed the hood, reached inside the wagon and switched on the lights, which then worked perfectly.

"Did I do something wrong?" Helen asked timidly.

"Just a loose connection," Craig muttered. "Take it easy driving home and you'll get there all right. Better have all the wiring checked first thing in the morning."

"In the car, baby," Helen said, depositing Peggy on the front seat. Peg scrambled to the far window and stared intently out at the dark. She seemed disappointed when Michael didn't appear, somewhat like a firefly, to justify her close attention.

"Better speak to her," Craig said in a low voice. "Or everyone in The Shades is going to get the impression that we have a family ghost on our hands."

"Don't we?" Helen replied.

Craig hung his head, looking tired and disgusted.

"If there's another explanation, I hope we won't be long in hearing it. But until then, I *saw* him tonight, and Peggy saw . . . Michael, and we weren't having the same nightmare. He did just disappear both times like a—like an apparition. Can you tell me what a little boy would be doing way out in the woods this time of the night, Craig?"

Craig started to speak, shook his head in resignation, then said, "I'll let *him* tell me. He's hiding, whoever he is. Maybe I can flush him out of the woods—"

Helen put a hand on his arm. "Don't stay around, Craig," she pleaded. "Please don't! Go home, or go to Amy's but get away from here."

"Helen, you're—"

"I'm scared silly," Helen finished for him, and she didn't care at all that Peggy was listening.

Eight

THE LAST BUSLOAD OF BOYS FROM THE GREENLEAF SCHOOL LEFT the campus at five-fifteen on the Saturday afternoon of the Old Settlers' Reunion, and Amy gratefully returned to her office to change into more casual clothes and lock up for the weekend.

Once she had dressed in hip huggers, a cashmere sweater and a red babushka, she took a small gift-wrapped package from a desk drawer, walked down the first-floor corridor of the school's administration building and knocked lightly at Craig's door. When he didn't respond right away, Amy opened the door herself and looked in.

He was asprawl in a leather armchair in one corner of the office, reading glasses halfway down his nose, and he was making rapid notes on a pad of paper. The only light in the office came from the Tensor lamp on a shelf above his head: he had drawn the blinds of the windows that overlooked the quadrangle of the Greenleaf School.

"We're supposed to meet Helen at five-thirty, remember?"

Craig blinked. "Now I do. I promise, I'll catch up to you on the midway." He noticed the birthday-wrapped package in her hand and said, "For Peg? What's the occasion?"

"No, it's something I picked up for Peter, one of those tricky interlocking wooden puzzles. I gave up trying to solve it after three days. Peter will solve it before bedtime, I'm sure."

"I thought he was getting out of the infirmary this afternoon."

"Mrs. Cagle says he's still running a temperature, and the

59

doctor won't OK his release. I feel so sorry for him, he'll miss the fun, and he desperately needs a little fun in his life." Amy opened her purse and took out a card. "Will you sign this? The gift will mean a whole lot more if it's from both of us."

"Sure." Craig put his signature on the card, then grinned sorrowfully. "This might mean he won't bother to open the present. Pete and I haven't been on the best of terms the past couple of weeks. In fact he's been pretty damned hostile. On the other hand, I've been too demanding, I think. But I expect a little more communication from a boy with his intelligence."

"You'll get it," Amy said. "Don't be discouraged."

"After almost a year I'm not even sure we're friends." Craig stared at the golden windows.

"If Dr. Tomlinson is satisfied with the progress you've made, then I think you should be. And I think you ought to put those notes away and come along. You could use a little fun yourself."

"I promise, Amy—another hour at the most."

Amy stood over Craig for a few moments; he looked sheepish and conciliatory so she bent to kiss him.

"I'm on my way," she said briskly. "But if I miss the fireworks on your account I'm going to be as uncommunicative as Peter Mathis for the next couple of weeks, bank on that."

After leaving Craig, Amy hurried upstairs to the second-floor infirmary, where Mrs. Cagle, the nurse on duty, greeted her.

"Is Peter asleep? I wanted to leave this with him; it's sort of a get-well-quick present."

"No, no, come in, Amy." They went through a screened doorway into the shadowy ward, which Peter Mathis had to himself that afternoon. He was sitting propped up in bed with a thermometer in his mouth, a small-boned nine-year-old with large brown eyes and an overgrowth of dark brown hair. He had flawless skin which was unusually white except for smudges under the eyes. Those eyes could hurt you, Amy had discovered upon first meeting Peter Mathis. Of all the boys at the school he was her favorite, but he was also the hardest to befriend, as Craig had observed.

"I hear you're feeling better," Amy said. Peter's expression didn't change. He watched Amy as narrowly as he had watched when she entered the ward. He undoubtedly had seen the gift in her hand, but it was not his style to demonstrate interest.

Amy put the little package on the bed near his hand. "Craig

picked this out," she lied. "He thought you'd enjoy working with it if you got tired of reading."

Peter stared at her with an intensity that some people took for rudeness, but Amy was used to that; she returned an unperturbed smile. "It might not be any fun," she suggested. "It's a puzzle, and it's awfully difficult; I couldn't work it myself."

She had said enough to interest him; his eyes flickered, taking in the beribboned package. Then Peter blinked, deliberately, thanking her.

Amy pointed to the present. "Let me know how you make out with that," she said jauntily. "I'll have to run now." She was not in quite the hurry that she pretended, she would have liked to spend a few more minutes with Peter, but his physical isolation in the lonely infirmary grieved her, and she knew of no way to cheer him up.

The main street of the village of The Shades had been closed and transformed into a three-block-long midway, at the east end of which the two dozen clanking rides and assorted thrill attractions of the Brinkley Brothers Carnival were twined in popping eye-watering blister-bright neon. Because the reunion was the traditional climax to the fall tourist season and because the night had turned fair and mild, both the midway and the carnival grounds were packed. Hap Washbrook had all his boys in harness and the Highway Patrol had sent over a couple of cars to keep traffic moving through the various detours, but Hap himself was not working too hard.

Earlier in the evening he had joined the foursome of Helen, Amy, Peg and Doremus, treated them to dinner at the fried-chicken booth run by the Women's Auxiliary of the VFW, then escorted them to the rides. There the two men left Amy and Helen behind and took the delighted Peggy for a whirl on the carousel.

"What are you in the mood for now, Peggy?" Hap asked, helping her down at the end of the ride; Peg looked around deliberately and then pointed at the rickety-looking Ferris wheel. Helen blanched, but Doremus took her hand and off they went.

"Oh, Lord," Helen muttered.

"Looks like a piece of junk," Hap conceded, "but I checked it out myself bolt for bolt. Amy, let's you and me grab the next seat."

One of his deputies, a tall youth with a slouch and a massive pearl-handled pistol on his hip, came up behind Hap and said in his ear, "Sheriff, Enoch says can you come down to the jail for a few minutes."

Hap scowled. "What for?"

"You got a phone call."

"Good Christ," Hap said. "I'm busy. Take a message."

"Enoch done that already."

Hap gave the deputy a suffering look and said patiently, "What was it?"

"He didn't tell me. Said to find you and ask can you come down to the jail. . . ."

Hap looked with genuine longing at the Ferris wheel, and then glanced regretfully at Amy. He said, loud enough to be heard over the cacophony of shrieks and wheeler-dealer carnival music, "Something I have to attend to, girls. I'll find you all in about ten minutes or so," and went striding off, with the deputy at his side.

Twenty-five minutes later he hadn't returned.

"No telling what's keeping him," Doremus said, when they got together following Peggy's third ride on the carousel. "But it could be something that'll have Hap tied up the rest of the evening."

He had been sitting in the unmarked patrol car for over an hour now, with the lights turned off and the radio turned off, and his eyes were stinging from the effort of focusing through powerful binoculars in an attempt to distinguish movement on either side of the brimming and turbulent Competition River, which gave the state park its name.

He was parked about a hundred yards from the designated meeting place and he had managed to drive into the park quietly, showing no lights, and find a well-concealed observation point, maneuvering his car by memory and the moon. He had felt confident that this was a good ploy and that sooner or later the one he had come to meet would become rattled or discouraged and give himself away. But just the opposite had occurred: Hap found himself restless and bored, and the feeling was growing on him that he'd been had.

He was so certain now that he'd been tricked by that phone call that he could admit he'd been uneasy in the beginning. So he had come creeping up the summit road and stopped a good distance away from the stony-sided rush of river and waited, waited to be sure in his bones that he had not been talking to a ghost.

The garbled amplified voices from below had ceased, and Hap looked at the luminous face of his chronometer, which gave the time as ten minutes to nine.

Be starting the fireworks soon.

Hap grunted and reached for the big six-battery electric torch clipped to the underside of the dashboard; his eyes shifted to the pump-action shotgun that always rode with him in the front seat.

"What for?" he asked himself, after serious thought about the need for such a weapon, but he was uneasy again and so he sprung the fully loaded shotgun from the clamp that held it upright and got out of the car, closing the door noiselessly behind him.

There was a satisfying crumpling sound overhead, and a violet smoky bloom. Hap turned his head for a look.

Get their money's worth this year, he thought. *Two thousand bucks just for fireworks.*

Whoosh!

Goddam beautiful, Hap thought, walking backward. *Really lights up the sky.*

He followed the river to the trail house, where the footbridge arched, trying to hear something besides the bubbling of the river. The house was securely padlocked as it should have been, tightly shuttered for the night. There were no surprises waiting.

I suppose I'll have to cross the bridge, he thought.

The sky crackled.

See it pretty good from up here.

Midway on the bridge he stopped and beamed his light down into the broken quarry of limestone, slab on slab, wet from the slashing river.

He glimpsed the thrown rock a second before it hit him, and he flinched just enough, getting his left arm up, to deflect it away from his face. It was a small rock but it stung his forearm, and he forgot all about the array of fireworks in the night sky.

Hurried probing with his light showed him nothing, and he never saw the second whizzing stone at all. It flicked off the bridge rail and shot away into darkness.

Hap figured he'd better get the hell off the bridge.

Crouching, he followed the beam of his torch to the far side and half slid down a slope of stone into a narrow space where the waters of the river lapped coldly at the soles of his boots.

A rocket boomed emphatically overhead, loosing a shower of crimson embers, and the stones that wedged the sheriff to the river glowed for a moment.

"All right, I'm here!" Hap shouted angrily. "Where are you?"

He thought he heard something downstream—a rock dislodged into water. He stepped out ankle deep into the tugging river and shot his light along the edge. The beam carried a good quarter of a mile, fading at last into the woods where the river began its fall.

"I've got a loaded shotgun here," Hap yelled. "And I'm using it."

His hearing was affected by the constant low roar of the river, but all the same he could not mistake the sound which seemed to come out of the darkness only a few inches behind his head, a terrible, animal sighing that shocked his heart still.

Something like a baseball bat swung with maniacal force hit him on the left arm just above the elbow, snapping the bone. Hap screamed and the shotgun clattered to the rocks at his feet. The force of the blow knocked Hap to one side and his feet slipped on the slightly pitched, slick-surfaced rock he'd been standing on. He fell, cracking the lens of his flashlight, and plummeted up to his chest in the numbing river.

The cold water helped him to recover from the first sickening burst of pain and he struggled to keep from being pulled along by the current. Somehow, without losing his grip on the flashlight, he managed to inch his way back up the slanted stone, to drag himself free of the river. With his right arm extended, Hap lifted the beam of the flashlight and saw, through a haze of pain, who had assaulted him. He was almost as shocked as he had been to hear Michael's voice over the telephone. For a few seconds he wasn't even aware of the fact that the shotgun he had dropped was now pointed at him.

"You loved my mother, didn't you? You sneaked around and you made love to her, but you wouldn't stand up for her!"

Hap scarcely heard him. He concentrated on not slipping into the river again, on finding a niche for his feet, on easing carefully to his knees. The pain in his broken arm was excruciating but he'd been in pain many times, he knew how to ignore it and set to work.

The sky was lighted once more, in tones of gold and strawberry pink, but there was a deadly roaring in his ears which cut out all sound. Hap had no definite plans, except to stand on his feet again. Nothing else seemed so important to him, not even the fact that he was in the company of an Imp of Death. But he had another look at the shotgun as he dragged himself up; to his horror there was a pinching in his stomach, a bitterness of dread.

"That tears a man up," he heard himself say. "Please God, don't shoot me with it." And he heard a skyrocket going up. The sky dissolved in streamers of green. There were earnest words in Hap's mind, on the tip of his tongue. It was an incredible feeling, being there with an Imp of Death, under the muzzle of his own gun, pinned by those long-dead and hating eyes: *it would never happen and morning would come along.* He would get out of bed at the usual time and put on the starched forest-green shirt with the big weight of polished badge and go down the street to Madge's place for his eye-opening cup of coffee, and it would be *Hello, Sheriff,* as usual. Another rocket whistled dismally. *See it good from up here,* Hap thought. He said hopelessly, humbly, choking on his words, "That thing tears a man up," and in the next instant his chest was ripped open by the double-aught shot, he followed his own sprayed blood out into the river, and disappeared.

With a final volley the sky went to black again, and the crowd on the picnic grounds that fronted the hundred-foot Competition Falls began to stir and think of the traffic jam that was to follow.

"Is that all?" Peggy said in an aggrieved voice, and Amy reached over to pat her knee.

"I don't think that was the grand finale," Helen said, wishing they weren't so close to the falls. It was a long way to the parking lot, and she had been on her feet for several hours. She wondered if Doremus would mind if she just leaned on him for a few minutes, and then she wondered if she wasn't a little giddy from fatigue.

"What's a grand finale?" Peggy asked.

Helen started to explain but the grand finale was under way, rockets' red glare and patriotic streamers of blue and white unfurling above the glowing falls.

Ahhhh, they all said, gratefully, and began to think of home, began to turn away.

And then the thing came down the falls, in a torrent of white water, came fast, slowed, turned, slipped past jutting ice-slick rocks, turned a little more, head lolling, arms flopping, was washed downward to a level a dozen feet above the deep foaming pool at the base of the falls.

Ahhhh ! they said, amazed, and they lingered to puzzle over this thing that seemed a joke, that could not be accepted for what it was obviously meant to be, a dead body, because the Old Settlers' Reunion had come to its customary reassuring end, and they were ready to go.

The thing in the falls hung motionless for several seconds on the ledge where it had dropped, and then the jetting pressure of water behind it pushed it gently forward, and for an instant before it plunged down into the floodlit pool it emerged from the curtain of white water in its shredded green shirt and the big handsome shotgunned badge on the shirt glittered. The vacant eyes of Hap Washbrook surveyed them all pensively.

"Oh, my God!" Helen said, and hid her face from the sight of Hap's cut-string sprawl into the deep river pool.

Nine

DOREMUS FINISHED HIS THIRD GLASS OF WHISKEY, FEELING pleasantly flushed in the warm kitchen. Helen sat as quietly as she had been sitting all evening. She had discovered it was useless trying to keep her thoughts away from the sight of Hap, so torn and pathetically loose-jointed, spilling madly down the sparkling falls. It was easier for her to breathe when she went over the tragedy many times. Repetition dulled the shock; the prospect of healing tears seemed less remote.

"Michael called Hap tonight, didn't he?" she asked Doremus, and the detective, after a moment's hesitation, nodded.

Helen felt a dolorous urge to laugh. "And then he killed Hap."

"I don't know what went on up there. Michael is just a voice on the telephone to me, so far."

"What did he say to Hap?"

"Only Hap knew. The deputy who took the call—Enoch, Enoch Mills; know him?—didn't have too much to tell."

"But it *was* Michael. Just a voice on the telephone, you say, but he can be anywhere, he can see anything, he wants to kill us!"

Doremus looked up sharply. "Why did you say that?"

Helen seemed shaken and lost.

"Has he threatened you? Was there a call you haven't told me about?"

"No . . ."

"Then why did you say he wants to kill you?"

"Because he must hate me! Because he . . . came back, and his mother wasn't there, she was dead . . . she died, she died in that place where I had her put away, and he blames me, he blames me, he always did and he—" Helen cut herself off with an anxious jerk of her head and stared helplessly at Doremus. "I have to stop thinking like that," she said softly.

Doremus studied her glumly, but he had nothing to say that might comfort her; he was too involved with the riddle of Michael Young. Presently he asked, as if he were thinking aloud, "How did Michael get along with Dr. Britton?"

"Get along . . . ? I don't think Michael saw much of him. Andy might have treated him once or twice for a cold or one of the usual childhood illnesses, but I don't remember specifically. I scarcely knew Andy myself in those days."

"Was Hap the sheriff then?"

"Yes." She didn't wait for Doremus to ask, but said immediately, "And Michael knew him a little better than he did Andy. On two occasions when Michael ran away he was found and handed down the line by state authorities, eventually reaching Hap, who always took the time to drive him home. Hap treated Michael very well, sympathetically. I'd say Hap went out of his way to befriend Michael. But of course none of us had any luck there."

"Suppose Michael was alive today—can you think of any reason why he'd want those two men dead?"

"Alive?" Helen said, startled. "Do you think—"

"I don't know what I think," Doremus replied patiently, "I'm just taking ideas out of the air. What about it, Helen?

I know the boy resented you, but what could he have held against Hap and the doctor? It could be a little thing, actually, warped out of proportion by the passing of time. People have been murdered for any number of petty reasons, and not always by the criminally insane. So if Michael— Wait a minute."

The detective's eyes glittered. "I could be asking the wrong question. It's not how they treated *him* that matters; it's how they treated his mother." He looked to Helen for confirmation, but she seemed bewildered. "Is there any chance that Dr. Britton could have been making love to your sister?"

"What an ugly— Of course not!"

"As far as you know. But he was well acquainted with Alice, and admittedly she had a lot of boyfriends. He could easily have been one of them. If he was and if it went on for any length of time, then his wife probably knew about it. I'll have to ask her."

"You couldn't ask Elsa something like that!"

"Yes, I could. I'm used to being indelicate."

"You certainly are," Helen said furiously, but her anger turned to mortification and she stared out into the dark again. Doremus seemed not to have noticed her remark. He said:

"Hap was a born womanizer, I know that for sure, and he wouldn't have overlooked someone as attractive as your sister."

"I don't think," Helen said in a strangled voice, "that it was just a . . . casual affair, although it probably started that way, for both of them. In the end Hap acted as if he loved her, despite all the trouble she caused him. He saw as clearly as I did that she had to have psychiatric care. He rode with me the day I took Alice to the sanitarium. He kept her laughing as long as he could, kept her from thinking about being locked up."

"So you and Hap made the decision to have your sister committed. And she had to be certified incompetent by a physician."

"Andy signed the papers."

Doremus said reflectively, "A psychotic personality might find that enough justification for killing the doctor—for arranging his death. Was your sister committed by court order?"

"Yes. The judge was a man named Schofield. But he died several years ago." Doremus looked questioningly at her. "I think it was a heart attack. He was a very old man." Helen came back to the table slowly and sat down, looking more intrigued than frightened. "I don't see how Michael could have survived that snowstorm. After all, his coat was found; I identified it. Bones were found. It couldn't have been some other little boy."

"As far as I know, there wasn't a medical examination to determine how long the remains had been in the open. There was no attempt to match the teeth in the skull with dental charts. Hap did a sloppy job. It could easily have been another boy, one who had wandered off from the Greenleaf School months or possibly years before Michael Young was lost. I don't think it would be too difficult to check that out. Your nephew could do it for me."

"I can't believe Michael is alive," Helen said stubbornly. "If he is, where has he been? How has he managed to live?"

"By his wits," Doremus suggested. "He wasn't a baby when he disappeared. From all I've heard, he was a boy with a lot of determination, and he knew the woods, he knew how to protect himself."

"What about the telephone calls, Doremus? That isn't a man calling. It's a little boy."

"That's one of the ways he scares me, with his elaborate playacting. Apparently he's worked this whole thing out carefully. It's significant that he called you first."

Helen looked at him uncomprehendingly.

"I'm sure it gave him a great deal of pleasure, settling up with the doctor and with Hap, but in a way they were incidental participants in the tragedy of his mother. You're the one who will have to suffer most for what happened to her. You came down here and meddled in their lives and sent the mother away to die. You're the one he came to hate with the kind of pathological bitterness that could eventually turn him into a murderer." Helen closed her eyes and looked momentarily ill.

"How can we find him?" she asked. "Before he calls, before he comes? I don't know if I can take—"

Doremus said gently, "In the morning I'll talk to Enoch Mills. From what I've seen of him he's a good policeman, and he has the authority as undersheriff to investigate anyone who could possibly be Michael Young, once I convince him he should. That will take time, and I'm not sure it will help. In the meantime it would be sensible to pack Peggy off to relatives."

Helen was silent. "I can't," she said eventually. "It would be better if we both went somewhere, for a few weeks, however long a time you need to find Michael."

"I'm sorry. You'll have to stay here, Helen."

"What do you mean?" she flared. "Stay and be killed? What kind of sense—"

"If you leave The Shades he's bound to follow, and there's no way I can protect either one of you then. But if you're here it's possible to arrange protection. On second thought, maybe Peggy had better stay; a deputy can keep an eye on her while she's at school without scaring Michael off. I don't want anything to divert his attention from you—and from me."

"What are you going to do?"

"I want to make it clear to Michael that if he tries to harm you in any way he'll have to kill me first." Doremus lighted the miniature cigar he'd been holding. "I think he'll accept the challenge."

"How do you know he'll try to kill you?"

"He'll have to, because I'll be with you twenty-four hours a day from now on." Helen frowned at this piece of news. "Because he's bright, he'll know why I'm sticking close to you and to Peg. Because he's been successful so far, he'll be eager to get on with it, to complete his revenge. I think I understand him well enough to know he won't be worried about me. And one mistake is all he needs to make."

"You're going to stay here?" Helen said, trying not to sound dismayed.

"I'd rather be on the ground floor," Doremus said obliviously.

"I don't think there's room—"

"Your office might be the best place for me; wasn't there some sort of couch in there? Let's have a look." He walked down the unlighted hall with Helen behind him. "What's that —cellar door?" He opened it, peered down the steps, then studied the lock on the door. "No good," he muttered. "Well, I can put a dead bolt lock on in the morning." He closed the door and went on. "That's a bathroom under the stairs, isn't it?"

"Half bath; there's no tub, and the shower isn't very—"

"All I need is a place to shave in the morning," Doremus said cheerfully, turning on the light in the foyer. He stopped in the office doorway and looked down at the clutter. The sofa he had referred to was a Victorian piece about five and a half feet long, rigidly padded.

"Perfect," Doremus said. "No windows; I like that."

"I suppose I could move some things out—"

"No need to go to any trouble; I'll be comfortable here. In the morning if you have time we might run over to my place for a few things."

"You can't sleep on that sofa; it would be like lying on a sidewalk all night."

"I only sleep when there's nothing else to do," Doremus said. "I noticed you had a fine antique chess set in the other room. I'll borrow it for a few nights if you don't mind."

Helen stared at him, hazily. "You're really staying, aren't you?"

"Is something wrong?"

"No. Oh, no."

"Sure I won't be in the way here?"

"We'll ... we'll manage. Business as usual."

Ten

NOT LONG AFTER DAWN AMY WAS HALF AWAKENED IN HER BED BY the sound of Craig's car outside. She rolled over, eyelids twitching, her hand groping. The part of the bed in which he had slept was still faintly warm. She reached for his pillow, hugged it tightly against her bare breasts, sighed and dropped off to sleep again.

The ringing of the telephone reawakened her.

Amy struggled upright. "Craig?" she said thickly, and then remembered she had heard him leaving. She glanced at the bedside clock; the time was seven-forty-five. "Why didn't you get me up?" she said crossly. The phone rang again. Amy popped her eardrums with a yawn, shuddered, reached for the receiver of the telephone.

"H'lo?"

"I want to talk to Craig."

"What?"

"Let me talk to Craig," the boy repeated.

"Craig . . ." Amy said, trying to get her bearings. "Craig isn't . . . it's eight o'clock in the morning; what makes you think he'd be here ? Who is this, please ?"

"He *was* there," the voice said deliberately. "He was sleeping right there with you. Where did he go ?"

"Are you calling from the school ?" Amy felt a chill that gripped her like jaws. "Who are you ?"

"Michael," he said emphatically, without hesitation, "and I want—"

"Michael ?"

". . . to talk to Craig."

"Michael Young ?" There was no sound on the line for several seconds. Amy felt as if she'd swallowed her tongue when she tried to speak. "What . . . Why do you want Craig ?"

"I have to tell him something," the boy said with great impatience.

"He . . . he really isn't here. I mean it, he left. I was half asleep, but I heard him drive away." Having admitted that much, Amy lost some of her shock and became cautious, realizing that she might indeed be talking to one of the more Machiavellian Greenleaf boys. She said boldly, "Prove you're Michael Young." The silence that followed was so long she was afraid he was going to hang up. But eventually he spoke again, in a voice that was mischievous, but with an underlying hint of malice.

"When my mother was a little girl, she was playing with Auntie Helen. They called their game 'beauty shop.' My mother cut all of Auntie Helen's hair off with scissors. It was red hair when she cut it, but when the hair grew out it changed color, to dark brown. Auntie Helen knows. Ask her."

"All right. That's . . . a good story, if it's true, and I will ask Helen." Amy was already certain that he had told the truth; she was now certain that this was Michael Young. "But do you have any more proof ?"

"I don't want to talk to you anymore," he said.

"Last night . . . something bad happened to Sheriff Washbrook. Do you know anything about it ?"

"I know," Michael said, his voice sullen.

"Were you there ?"

"He got what he had coming. Would you put Craig on ?"

Amy said desperately, "Michael, where are you now ? I'd

like to come and see you."

"I told you, I *don't* want to talk to you!" Michael cried.

"Please listen to me. Craig isn't here. But if there's something you wanted to tell him, then tell me, and I'll find him right away."

Amy thought she had demanded too much, but then he said, in a voice that seemed to be fading, "Tell him . . . I wish he was dead."

"Oh, no. No, Michael. You don't mean that."

"I wish he was dead. I hate him."

"You can't hate everyone, Michael. You just can't! Craig was good to you, he took care of you. . . ." She caught her breath, and listened incredulously. He was weeping. "Michael," Amy continued, "I do want to help you. Please tell me where you are, and I'll come right away."

He sobbed again. "I'm—" he started to say, and then the connection was broken.

"Oh, God, what am I going to *do*?" Amy said brokenly, but she'd already half made up her mind, so she finished her cigarette and dressed hurriedly, in slacks and a ski sweater, and, forgetting about work, she went out into the chilly mist-bright morning to the ramshackle garage for her car.

Doremus asked her to go over the telephone conversation with Michael four times, until he was satisfied that he had it nearly word for word. When Helen left them alone in the kitchen to greet an early-rising antique hound Doremus asked bluntly, "Why did he call your house looking for Craig?" Amy reddened. "Oh well, what time did Craig leave, then?"

"I don't know," Amy mumbled. "It was light outside. He might have left as early as six-thirty, or as late as seven-thirty. I heard his car, but I didn't really wake up."

Helen came back and poured fresh coffee for the three of them. "How are we going to tell Craig?" she asked.

Doremus said, "I don't think he should be told."

"But Michael threatened to kill him!" Amy protested.

"No, he didn't. Not according to what you told me. Michael said, 'Tell him I wish he was dead.' That isn't a threat."

"As far as *I'm* concerned it is. And he also said he hated Craig."

"Supposing he does."

"Well, doesn't that mean he intends—"

Doremus shook his head. "I don't know why he called you; it wasn't what I expected. But what Michael had to say doesn't change my mind about him. I still believe he intends to murder Helen next."

Amy almost dropped her coffee cup and she gave Helen a startled look. Helen smiled wanly and explained while Doremus industriously buttered half a pastry and ate it.

"Michael's alive?" Amy said, staring at Doremus. "Well, now, if you'll pardon my saying so, *that's* incredible."

" 'Ghosties and beasties and things that go bump in the night' you believe in, but a rational explanation defeats you."

"Rational, ha! Your 'explanation' simply explains away too much. What about the little boy everyone has seen? Peggy saw him twice, and poor Elsa. . . . Also, I talked to a boy on the telephone this morning, not a man."

"A man mimicking a ten-year-old boy," Doremus suggested.

"No, sir," Amy said stubbornly. "I work with boys that age, I listen to them eight or ten hours a day. I'm not about to be fooled by an impersonation. The voice I heard was genuine."

Helen nodded. "I agree with Amy. I don't know if we heard the same voice, but I'm convinced—"

"Anyone can be fooled over the telephone," Doremus objected.

"I asked him to prove he was Michael Young," Amy said, "and he did."

Doremus looked at her with renewed interest. "Something you forgot to tell me?"

"Yes. After I asked him to give me proof there was a long silence, and then he said, in a sort of smart-alecky way—you know how they are at that age—oh, God! he said that when Helen and her sister were little girls they liked to play 'beauty shop.' Beauty shop. And one time Alice took a pair of scissors and cut almost all of Helen's hair off. Her hair had been red, but when it grew back it had changed color, to dark brown."

An odd expression crossed Helen's face. "That's perfectly true. My parents made a terrible fuss about the hair-cutting, although it didn't matter very much to me. Alice was delighted, I think—there was always this rivalry between us. But I doubt if I've ever told anyone about that incident."

Craig came that night and listened stonily as Amy repeated the details of the telephone call from Michael. To her dismay he said nothing but looked at her as if she were lying, or losing her mind. Then Doremus took over and explained that he thought Michael was still alive. Craig was immediately interested, and unargumentative. He asked a great many questions, becoming more excited by the minute, so much so that he got up and began pacing restlessly the length of the kitchen.

"That's it," he muttered. "That has to be what happened! Michael lived through the blizzard. I'll start checking our records tonight to see if there was a boy missing from the school about the time my brother disappeared. Have you asked Enoch Mills to go through the sheriff's files on missing persons?"

Doremus nodded. "Mills drew a blank, but that isn't necessarily significant. Missing children often go unreported."

"Maybe Michael did survive," Amy said sharply to Doremus, not caring what Craig would think, "but there's still a little boy involved in all this. I don't see how you can deny that, or ignore it!"

Amy had halfway made up her mind that Doremus was a bumbler, and she wasn't prepared for the look he gave her. His eyes had a wolfish glint in them. Amy was suddenly aware of a formidable strength in this man which she had previously overlooked. She was, despite herself, intrigued by her discovery.

"I haven't ignored anything," he said quietly, "but for now all I can do is wait. And hope I haven't made any serious mistakes in judgment."

About two o'clock in the morning Helen came wide awake in her bed, icily certain that her room had been entered.

The sky outside was veiled with clouds and heavily tarnished by the yellow moon; the shadow of a tree loomed mothlike on one wall of the room. She saw a gliding figure near the bed and almost cried out.

"Mother," Peggy said plaintively, "I don't feel very good. I've got a stomachache."

Helen let her breath out a notch at a time and got up to help her daughter. She was wide awake by the time she returned to her room. The thought of strong hot coffee pushed her back into the hall.

Helen had thought it might be possible to sneak downstairs and invade the kitchen without being detected by Doremus;

she was halfway down the stairs without having made a sound at all, as far as she knew, when the door of the office opened and Doremus stepped out, pistol in hand. The high-intensity lamp behind him was masked, revealing only the square battlefield of the chessboard he had been studying.

"Could you make enough for two?" he asked her.

When the coffee was ready Helen carried it to the office on a tray. He was hunched over the ornately manned chessboard again; the black Colt pistol was only inches away from his left hand.

"Are you playing yourself?" Helen asked.

"No. These are my men here. Black belongs to a man named Arshenko, a Russian philologist at the Moscow University. We've been playing for years, ever since I met him at the University of Chicago. Play by mail now. I've only beaten him once in four years, but I think . . . I've got him now. I should know by next spring." He looked up, accepting a cup of the steaming coffee. "I don't suppose you play?"

"My husband and I used to play once in a while, but I—"

"Great!" Doremus enthused, sweeping the pieces from the board. "Would you care for a game right now?"

"What about Mr. Arshenko?"

"He can wait; I still have three days to decide on my next move." He began setting up the game. Helen thought of her bed upstairs, and sighed inaudibly. "I suppose one game . . . I'm really not very expert at this."

She proved it by losing to him within twenty minutes. Doremus then went over every mistake she had made in painstaking detail. Eventually a yawn burst out of her. Doremus looked in amazement at the clock on the desk.

"You really did very well," he said. "I think you have an aptitude for this game. My wife never could learn . . ." He reached for a cigar, discovered he had smoked the last one and sat back, staring disconsolately at the chessboard. Helen was putting the coffee cups back on the serving tray and she glanced at him, then felt moved to ask:

"When did your wife die, Doremus?"

"Three years ago."

"Her name was Marian."

"Yes. That's right." He was silent, but he looked up at Helen thoughtfully. "You've put up with this very well, my moving in and all. I know it hasn't been easy for you. But

76

there's no other way. I have to be here."

"I understand."

"He might not come . . . but if he does, you wouldn't have a chance alone. Marian never had a chance. She put up a fight, but what chance did she have?" His expression was cold, brooding.

Helen felt shocked by his words, but she couldn't make herself ask Doremus what had happened to his wife. His tension lessened, however, and he began to speak again.

"I had to fly out to Des Moines to bring back a suspect in a labor shooting. Usually when I was to be away overnight Marian drove to my sister's and stayed with them, but she was helping with a neighbor's wedding and she felt that she couldn't leave. She felt safe enough, and with reason: it was a fine spring week and the neighborhood was a good one, but is any neighborhood good enough?"

"We landed at Meigs Field at four in the morning and it was six by the time I booked my prisoner, almost seven when I reached home. The milkman and I arrived about the same time, so I put the milk in the refrigerator and glanced at the front page of the *Tribune* before going upstairs. There was no sign of forced entry—I would have noticed—the house was just as it should be. So I wasn't prepared at all, I just walked in on it." His eyes stung him; he rubbed them before continuing. "What struck me first was the quantity of blood on the walls; it still seemed fresh, but that was the trick of the sun coming through the blinds, I suppose. The room was devastated. I found Marian behind the bed, I mean jammed between the headboard and the wall. He'd finally broken the blade of his knife after stabbing her half a hundred times."

Helen, in the doorway, had turned a dull shade of gray, but her eyes were wide and filled with pity for him.

Doremus, hardly aware of her, went on inexorably. "The kid was in the bathroom; that was as far as he'd been able to travel. I don't know what she fought back with, fought the knife with, but I'd taught her the use of her hands and feet, I'd taught her a few alley things, and she had courage. He was a neighborhood kid we'd both tried to help. Probably she'd opened the door to him—that's the only explanation I have to this day. He was on the floor of the bathroom because he couldn't walk at all. Some of the blood on the walls was his. He had a scalp-rip and one empty eyesocket, reamed out, no expression on his face, it was hard and stiff like a mask, about an eighth of an inch of coagulated blood covered most of his face but he was conscious and breathing and he could talk. He cursed me when I walked in. I didn't think about what I was doing, or what I wanted to do. I just took out my service revolver and shot him five or six times and walked out again."

Helen could find nothing adequate to say; she took the tray to the kitchen, washed the cups and saucers, put everything away and then returned. Doremus was methodically aligning pieces on the chessboard again. He looked up with a strained smile.

"I didn't mean to bother you with all that."

"When have you had the chance to talk about it?"

"I don't think I've talked about it at all. I didn't know I could."

"You've kept to yourself much too long," Helen said reprovingly. They looked at each other for several moments, cautiously, almost friends. Then Doremus smiled again and reached for his glasses. "I enjoyed the coffee. Maybe we'll have a chance for another game of chess."

"Yes, I'd like that. Doremus . . . I'm afraid I haven't been particularly gracious the last couple of days. I apologize for that. I'm glad you're here, very glad. And not just because of Michael. I hope when this is over with, you'll feel like coming back for an evening now and then."

"Peg offered me half of her allowance if I'd stay on permanently," Doremus said innocently, and Helen, after turning red, laughed with him.

"She would. Good night, Doremus."

Eleven

ALTHOUGH DOREMUS WAS CONSIDERABLY LESS TROUBLE THAN THE average house guest, Helen soon discovered that having a full-time bodyguard and watchman was a strain on her nerves. By Saturday she was ready to jump at any excuse to get out of the house for a couple of hours, without Doremus tagging along; a PTA get-together at The Shades School seemed to offer a perfect opportunity, but she had to argue for almost an hour before Doremus grudgingly conceded she ought to be safe there without him.

"It's in the gym; there'll be three hundred people there!"

"That's what I don't like about it."

"One of them could be Michael, is that what you're thinking? He wouldn't dare try anything."

Doremus looked gloomily at the stub of his cigar. "I said you could go. Keep Peggy with you at all times."

"Of course I will."

"Park your car as close to the gym as you can, and it would be a good idea if you asked one of your friends to follow you home after the party; you don't have to explain why."

"All right," Helen said resignedly, wondering if she was going to enjoy her night out as much as she had anticipated.

"Call me if—"

"You remind me of my father!"

"I'll shut up," Doremus said, with a sardonic grin.

With the house to himself, Doremus took a leisurely hot shower, put on fresh Levi's and a favorite Pendleton shirt and walked outside.

After five minutes or so he became convinced that he was alone, and so he returned to the house, turned off the porch light and settled down in the office with an exemplary western novel. He was thoroughly absorbed in the fortunes of the Zachary family when the telephone rang.

Doremus looked up without much interest, then went back

to *The Unforgiven*. The phone continued ringing. When he counted eight rings Doremus put the book down and rose. By the tenth ring he was certain that whoever was calling expected him to answer.

"Connellys'," he said gruffly.

"You want to see me, don't you?"

Several seconds passed before Doremus answered; there was a chilly grin on his face. "That's right, kid."

"You can see me half an hour from now at the gristmill on Hawke's farm."

"Half an hour. Is that when you materialize, or whatever it is you do?"

"And you'd better come alone, or you won't see me."

The connection was broken, before Doremus could think of some way to keep him talking. He replaced the receiver and looked thoughtfully at his wristwatch. The time was a few minutes after nine. The boy had spoken quickly and sharply, as if he were as tired of waiting for a confrontation as Doremus himself. "That old gristmill?" Doremus said, half-aloud. "Don't you think you're stacking the odds, kid?" He reached for the telephone again, and dialed the home of Enoch Mills.

"This is Doremus," he said, when he had the undersheriff of The Shades on the line. "I just heard from Michael Young." He remembered then that the boy had not identified himself, but he went on: "I'm being set up for something, but I'm not sure what. . . . Yes, I probably could use some help. Helen Connelly took Peggy to some sort of school affair about an hour ago; I think it would be smart to send one of your deputies down there to keep an eye on her, without attracting a lot of attention. Now, I'm supposed to be at the gristmill on Hawke's farm in . . . approximately twenty-five minutes, and I'll be there all right. No, I don't want that. Give me, say, an hour, and then come in full throttle. I can stay alive that long no matter what, and I want him to feel secure enough to show himself."

The gristmill on Ironwall Creek had been built in the 1840's and was still operable, although it now served primarily as an out-of-the-way attraction for tourists with cameras looking for picturesque antiquities, and as a subject for local painters. It was located a hundred feet upstream from an unpaved farm road and at night was all but invisible, surrounded by massed trees at the water's edge.

After pulling his scooter off the road Doremus found the creekside path with the beam of his flash-light and started toward the mill. In his left hand he carried the nine-shot automatic.

Buckbrush slowed him down, but he was not overanxious to begin with. When he was sure he could find his way without falling into the water, he continued without a light until the mill wheel rose above him.

There was a padlock on the door but it hung oddly from the hasp, as if sheared by bolt cutters. Doremus, feeling cold and naked in the clearing, lifted one foot and kicked the door in. A moment later he went inside like a snake, rolled clear of the visible doorway, rose to his knees in the protective blackness, his lungs aching, his hands steady. He could see nothing at all. The mill smelled old, it smelled like rotting grain and rats. He moved cautiously and silently to his right.

Somewhere in the darkness a child giggled, muffling the sound with his hands, or his sleeve. Doremus froze, his thumb on the push button of the flashlight.

"All right," he said, not loudly, "I'm ready to talk, and I'd like to see you." He moved again, swiftly this time, on hands and knees. There was no flooring, at least where he was. He heard a tentative scurrying close by, in the loose dirt, but ignored it. He was listening for the sound of something human.

The child giggled again, openly, delightedly.

Doremus scrambled up, switching on the full beam of the light. The beam traveled in a wide blinding arc, past rough cut wooden columns, over a grinding stone, and pinned the sneaker-clad boy on the landing of a flight of stairs.

The startled boy lifted his hands, trying to shut out the glare, which was equal to that of a locomotive's headlight at short range. Doremus shielded his own eyes with an upthrust arm and began closing in. But the boy recovered quickly, turned his back and bounded up the stairs, too fast for Doremus, who tried to track him with the light.

At the foot of the stairs Doremus stopped, aiming the beam upward. He heard no sound, but dust was drifting down, as if someone were walking cautiously just above.

"Michael!"

He began climbing, pausing on every other step. The light was a powerful weapon, but he had lost his advantage and knew it. The sight of the boy had astonished him; he had expected almost anything else. . . . "I don't want to play games, Michael!" Doremus called. "I just want to talk to you." He reached the landing, where the stairs made a sharp angle to the left. Here the advantage became Michael's. But there was no choice except to go on.

He was halfway to the second floor of the mill when the heavy pitchfork came down, almost straight down, dropped but apparently not thrown. It struck Doremus' right wrist, and he let go of the light. He was not quick enough to seize the light before it fell through a space between steps and dropped to the ground below. Doremus recovered and fired three shots in a random pattern, intended to frighten and not to wound the boy he was chasing. Then he stumbled up the last of the steps in the dark, ran into a wall, stopped there and waited, breathing harshly.

"Your turn," he said, when he had caught his breath.

The boy giggled, sounding a little short of breath himself.

Doremus flexed the fingers of his right hand, reached into the pocket of his shirt and withdrew a pencil flashlight. He heard the giggling again; this time the boy seemed closer, but the sound was muffled and it was impossible to be certain. Doremus was tempted to use the tiny light immediately, but he had no more surprises to offer and he didn't want to waste that one.

While he waited his eyes adjusted to the dark. A little moonlight seemed to be filtering in, perhaps through cracks in the roof or the plank walls. Doremus edged forward, fingertips on the rough wall. The floor under his feet creaked and he stopped. A few seconds later the floor creaked again, but not from his weight. He reached out with his right hand; the wall ended, and there was a space. He felt a chill at the nape of his neck. Door space? he wondered. Was there a room beyond, and was the boy hiding there? He thought about the pitchfork that had come heavily down inches from his head, and he suppressed a shudder. But he took no more time to consider the possible danger; instead he switched on the pencil flashlight, stepped boldly into the space and pointed the beam.

The boy was standing about ten feet away, and for two or three seconds he was mesmerized by the light, his mouth open, a dull puzzled gleam in his eyes. Then he bolted, and vanished.

Doremus shifted the automatic to his right hand and made a

blind lunge for the boy, grasping the sleeve of his coat momentarily. But the boy twisted free; in the next instant Doremus was hit solidly in the back of the head and he pitched forward to the floor, stunned.

Now what the hell? he thought, and tried to get up, but only his mind was working—working him up into a panic. He had no idea whether he was still holding onto the automatic, but he tried to roll over on his back. The effort caused him to lose consciousness for several seconds. He awoke with a sickening pain in his skull, feeling helpless and condemned. Somewhere there was movement. Instinctively he sought to protect himself: he turned his head and raised an arm as a searing liquid poured down, soaking him to his toes. The fumes in his nostrils had the effect of ammonia.

Gasoline, he thought, groping, trying to balance himself on his feet. *Gasoline !* He coughed and struggled to keep his dripping hands away from his eyes, which had begun to burn frightfully from the fumes and from the gasoline trickling down his forehead. He groaned aloud.

There was a wavering, orange-yellow light outside the room, showing him the location of the doorway. Doremus, seeing the opening dimly, plunged toward it. Then he stopped in horror.

Michael stood outside, facing him impassively. He held a burning torch in one hand.

Doremus retreated instantly, clawing at the buttons of his sodden shirt. When he failed in his efforts to unbutton the shirt he tore it from his body. But the gasoline was still wet on his skin, it singed his skin delicately and suggestively.

"Now listen, boy," he said, backing away, "you're going to burn us both up with that thing. Don't come any closer." Michael seemed not to hear. He advanced carefully, a step at a time, his eyes solemn.

"Damn it, the fumes will ignite!" Doremus yelled, still retreating. "Now put that torch out, stomp it out quick, you hear me!" He could feel the wall behind his back and he edged sideways. Michael hesitated, seeming mildly uncertain about what he was doing. Then he smiled and came on, more quickly, holding out the torch. His lips trembled, as if he were trying to speak.

Doremus threw himself back against the wall, since there was no place else for him to go. The torch was close enough for him to feel the heat of it.

"*No!*" he shouted.

Behind him dry boards splintered and popped like fire-crackers, giving way; he toppled out of range of the bright curling torch in the boy's hand, and cried out fearfully, shocked by weightlessness, by a rush of cold air. The side of the gristmill appeared to leap away from him, recede into darkness. Doremus had a confused impression of sky and circling trees and then, luckily for him, he plunged head down into the placid waters of the millpond.

By the time he managed to paddle ashore, covered with slime and still redolent of gasoline, he was exhausted and shaking. He lay in the weeds and leaves for several minutes, half un-conscious, until he heard voices. Then he made the necessary effort to pull himself all the way out of the water. Trembling and sick to his stomach, he staggered and crawled as far as the clearing in front of the mill, where a light flashed on him.

"Just hold it right where you are, mister, we've got two shotguns here!"

"Did you see him?" Doremus mumbled. "Is he still in there? Where's the boy?"

A third man came crashing through the buckbrush. "What have you got here, Pa?"

"Just some crazy old bum, Willis," Hawke muttered. "All right, you, get walking."

"I'm trying to explain," said Doremus, standing his ground, "that there was a little boy here just a few minutes ago. *He's* the one who tried to set fire to your mill . . . set fire to me too. He's about ten years old; dark hair, fair skin. He was wearing sneakers. I don't know where he went but we've got to find him!"

The other son scratched his cheek and said to Doremus, "A little boy, huh?"

"That's right, did you see him?"

"Coulda been a little boy I saw hightailing across the meadow two—three minutes ago. Didn't get a good look."

"Which way was he headed?" Doremus asked eagerly.

"North. Toward the Overmeyers' place. Pa, you figure there's any truth in what he's saying?"

Doremus explained who he was, naming Enoch Mills as a reference, and Mr. Hawke seemed a little less inclined to give him both barrels on the spot. "Well," he drawled, "I guess it won't hurt to go along with you far as the Overmeyers'. Jack, you and Willis look in the mill see if there was any damage done. Willis, give this man your jacket so he don't freeze to death."

"It's my new jacket, Pa."

"He ain't gonna to steal it. Come with me, mister, and you two watch out for yourselves."

Gratefully buttoning up the fleece-lined jacket he had borrowed, Doremus followed the farmer, who had a light of the type Doremus had taken with him into the barn. They made good time to the crest of the meadow, and there, in full moonlight, they paused to study the landscape. There was not even a cow in sight.

"That's the Overmeyer place," Hawke said, pointing.

"Who owns the property down by the road there?"

"Man named Brunell. Artist of some sort; don't know him well." He turned toward the Overmeyer farm. "Reckon this the way we ought to go, but it don't seem like much use."

"Why not split up?" Doremus suggested. "The boy might have headed toward Brunell's; there are a lot of trees for cover down there."

"Yehp, but if he knows this pasture he wouldn't have run that way—gets real marshy for about fifty yards below that old barn."

"He might not know the pasture though. I think I'll have a look at Brunell's. Borrow your light?"

"What? Oh, take it, otherwise you'll have mud all over Willis' good jacket. Mister, I hope this is worth all the trouble."

"It's worth it," Doremus said, and he started rapidly down the slope of the pasture while Hawke walked off toward the other farm. With the powerful light it was easy for Doremus to avoid the worst of the marsh when he came to it, and once he had crossed the marsh he found easy going to the big peaked barn above.

The property seemed deserted. There was a light in the small house a hundred yards away, close to the road, but no dogs came barking and no animals stomped restlessly in the barn at his approach. Looking up, Doremus had an inkling why. There was a large skylight, facing north, on one wing of the roof.

He killed his light and moved closer to the barn, staying in shadow. The great front doors of the barn were securely chained shut, but there was a sign next to them. Doremus masked his light with his hand and turned it on the sign.

BRUNELL GALLERIES, it said. PLEASE ENTER AT THE BACK.

Doremus looked over one shoulder at the house. For an instant he saw someone silhouetted in the single lighted window. Near the house the woods were thick, a likely hiding place, if Michael had come this way. Chances were he was half a mile gone by now, gaining all the time. . . .

Inside the barn there was a spate of noise, a curious, flat, metallic clashing.

Doremus slipped around to the side of the barn and walked past small darkened windows, a dozen or more, until he reached a conventional door with flagstones in front of it. There was another sign but he didn't stop to ponder it, because the door was standing open. He opened it a little more and stepped inside, switching on the flashlight as he did so. The first thing he saw was an enormous, seal-like bronze nude on a granite pedestal four feet high. Behind her there were other seals—or women, but what they were wasn't immediately apparent—and then a spindly forest of cold-steel men, some walking, some running, some kneeling. And beyond those, stretching on for what seemed like a city block, were globs and thickets of metal, odd-shaped baskets and geometric figures of dazzling complexity, all done in copper wire, or jagged black spokes.

Doremus lifted his light and discovered a gallery overhead, then a congeries of brightly painted metal pieces, all hanging on nearly invisible wires from the high rafters.

One of the mobile sculptures was moving, its cleaver parts trembling, brushing together.

He shifted the angle of his light and saw the hiding muddy boy at the top of the stairs to the gallery. The boy's eyes looked dark and glazed; they scarcely blinked as he turned his head and stared into the flashlight beam. He was breathing hard.

Doremus sighed. "OK; come down."

The boy leaped suddenly, away from the light. In his haste he brushed against a spindly column and a fierce white head fell to the gallery floor, rolled, plummeted toward Doremus. He stepped aside quickly, almost tripping, and grabbed a plaited plastic rope for support. Above his head a bell tolled, deeply, momentously.

"Then I'll come up," Doremus said, and he started up the flight of stairs, raking the gallery with his light. The bell tolled slowly, three times more. The boy backed away. Doremus kept the beam of the lamp low, not wanting to blind him.

"Time to quit running . . . Michael."

The boy ran anyway, darting among the groupings of statuary on the gallery floor. Doremus stalked him. Each time the boy paused for breath the light touched him, inspiring a new frenzy, a new leap. He was like a hounded animal, Doremus thought, and despite the fact that this boy had tried to set him on fire, Doremus felt genuinely sorry for him.

"Easy now, I won't hurt you."

Sobbing, the boy crouched at the edge of the gallery floor, underneath the rail.

"Don't try it," Doremus warned, closing slowly. The bell tolled and the boy glanced fearfully at the barn floor, twenty feet below.

The bell tolled for the eleventh or twelfth time; the boy jerked suddenly, stared in astonishment at Doremus, teetered wildly, lost his balance and started to fall. But as he went over the edge, his windmilling hands seized the iron railing and he swung there precariously. Doremus dived, threw an arm around his waist and hauled him back to the gallery floor. The boy fought him furiously, escaped, stumbled and ran for the stairs. As Doremus got to his feet the lights in the barn flashed on. He limped toward the stairs. Two men had entered the barn. One of them was a burly, bald artist type with an improbable beard. The other man was Craig Young, who was holding the weeping unresisting boy in his arms and looking up at Doremus with an incredulous expression.

"Good, you got him," Doremus muttered, starting down.

"Peter?" Craig said to the boy. "Peter, what's the trouble, what are you doing here? How did you get here?"

"Do you know who he is? Doremus said, scowling.

"Of course I know him. He's one of our boys. His name is Peter Mathis."

"I think he's the one who's been playing Michael on the telephone . . . and there's no end to his versatility: he tried to kill me tonight."

"That's impossible," Craig said angrily.

"Is it? Let *him* tell you."

"I don't know what he's doing this far from the school, but I know he hasn't been making any telephone calls. Not Peter."

"No? Why are you so sure?"

"Because Peter is mute," Craig said curtly, comforting the terrified boy.

Twelve

WEARING A PAIR OF PAINT-DAUBED DUNGAREES AND A CLEAN IF tattered shirt borrowed from the sculptor Brunell, Doremus sat in the office of the Greenleaf School's headmaster. He was barefoot, his shoes having been too dirty for the velvety blue carpet, and his neck was stiffening from the plunge into the millpond, but Enoch Mills had provided him with a good cigar and he felt as if he would get through the night without too much difficulty.

"Peter couldn't have left the grounds this afternoon without being missed," the headmaster insisted. His name was Quinlan and he had the vestigial crispness of an ex-military man, though his face was lapped and folded from age, and his lips trembled when he wasn't speaking.

"Saturday's a free day at the school, ain't it?" Enoch Mills asked. "A good many of the boys go into town."

"Usually, Sheriff. But we played a football game here this afternoon, so all but a handful of the boys stayed on the campus. The others were in the company of parents or relatives."

"Could one of Peter's roommates have doubled for him during the bed check?"

"We're familiar with that ruse," the headmaster said, smiling faintly. "Also, Peter doesn't have a roommate."

"I'd like to have a look at the hall where he lives," Doremus said.

"Certainly. I'll take you there myself." The headmaster unlocked a drawer of his desk, took out a set of keys and accompanied Mills and Doremus across the misty quadrangle.

The bell in the tower of the administration building tolled twice as the headmaster unlocked the door of Dobbs Hall. The entrance was well lighted and clearly visible from the gatehouse. Inside there was a single bright light at each end of the corridor.

They went up stairs to the top floor, where Peter Mathis

lived. There was another, simpler lock on the door of the suite. Quinlan let them in with a passkey.

"Each suite contains two bedrooms and a study room," the headmaster whispered as they entered. "Let's see . . . I believe Peter has this room." They walked through a curtained doorway into a cubicle which contained two barracks-style beds and two dressers, nothing more. One bed was bare to the mattress. The other looked as if it had been slept in, at least briefly.

Doremus felt a draft on his stiff neck and went to the dormer windows. There were three of them, casement-type windows twenty-four inches wide. One window had been cranked open as far as it could go. The ledge outside was granite, about eight inches deep. He looked down at the quadrangle forty feet below. Some of the stones of the wall protruded unevenly for an inch or so, but there were no secure handholds.

Doremus turned his head carefully to the right. The roof slanted outward, past the windows, and where it ended there was a metal rain trough that looked dependable. He put one foot on the ledge and tried to get through the window space, but, thin as he was, he couldn't make it. He stuck his head out as far as possible and surveyed the gray-and-red slate roof.

"Peter couldn't have gone out that way," the headmaster protested, "it's far too dangerous. All the boys know it. We lecture them every year on the dangers of trying to climb—"

"I'm sure most of them take the lectures to heart, but this boy is something else again. I believe he went out this way, and came back this way, not once but as many as a dozen times. Let's go down."

From the quadrangle Doremus located Peter's window.

"If he could negotiate the slate to the point where the roof flattens, then he could walk across the buildings without difficulty. I doubt that anyone would see him against the background of the ridge. The hard part would be the first twelve feet—or the last, if he's returning to his room. With the rain trough to stand on and sneakers for grip he might make it easily to the flat of the roof. I wouldn't care to try it myself though. Let's find a way for him to climb down, now that we've got him up there."

They walked to the end of the second dormitory. Here Doremus saw a door in the otherwise blank wall, and a covered walkway to the cafeteria. Ivy grew thickly on the rugged facing of the wall.

"Reckon he clumb down that ivy?" Mills said, looking dubious.

"It's the only way off the dormitory roof. Not such a bad climb; the roof of the walkway there is a couple of floors high."

"Peter Mathis isn't a particularly strong or athletic youngster," Quinlan said, his voice thin and doleful. "What could have possessed him to do such a dangerous thing?"

Doremus looked thoughtfully at the headmaster. "Maybe Craig can help us here. Let's find out how the boy is."

Craig and Amy had come downstairs from the infirmary and were sitting on opposite ends of the couch in the headmaster's office.

"He's asleep now," Amy said as soon as the men came in. "It wasn't easy; the sedative we gave Peter should have knocked him out in a matter of minutes, but he was so horribly disturbed . . ." Her voice was bleak. "He couldn't stop threshing in the bed, and moaning. I don't know when I've spent a worse half hour." Craig had no comment. He looked aghast, demoralized. He was trying to smoke a cigarette, but his hand shook so badly that the effort made him look almost comical, like a talentless actor miming a drunk.

"Will we be able to ask Peter some questions in the morning?" Enoch Mills said tentatively, and Craig said, flaring:

"Absolutely not!"

After a few seconds he apparently regretted his tone and looked up at them with a trace of apology. "Peter is badly in need of rest, and . . . and complete quiet. It might be necessary to keep him tranquilized for several days. You see, I don't have a clear idea of the trauma he's suffered, and I won't until I've had the opportunity to sit down with him and—"

Doremus said, "Could Peter Mathis be Michael, your brother?"

The psychologist winced as if he'd said something deliberately foolish. "What are you talking about?"

"Let me put that another way. Could he *think* he's your brother?"

"Good God, of course not!"

"Originally you believed that the boy who was telephoning Helen had convinced himself he was Michael Young."

"Yes, I thought that was a possibility. But Peter doesn't know anything about my brother! Oh, I'm sure during the past couple of weeks he's heard the gossip about 'Michael's ghost,' all that nonsense—I must be quite a figure of fun around here because of it. But Peter hasn't been doing any telephoning. I've told you that already."

"Yes, he's mute. But his problem is psychological, isn't it, and not physical."

"He stopped speaking when he was about four years old, because of extreme emotional problems, and he hasn't said a word since."

"Tell me about Peter. Where's he from?"

"St. Louis. His childhood has been . . . totally grim. His mother was a spoiled and hateful young woman. At seventeen she became pregnant, refused to marry her lover and settled down in her parents' home to wait for the birth of the baby. The girl apparently was having her revenge on unloved parents, and if you met them you'd know why they were unloved. They're old, rich, prominent, and as heartless a pair as I've ever seen. I don't know if it's to their credit that they refused to be intimidated by their daughter's action. They simply retired to their mansion, seeing no one. Even today they seldom appear in public. So Peter was born, and grew up in an atmosphere of scathing hatred. One thing in the mother's favor: apparently she was fond of Peter, she looked after him herself. But she burned to death smoking in her bed when Peter was three and he was left on his own, totally vulnerable. I've already said he stopped speaking at the age of four, which may give you an idea of what he suffered at the hands of those people." Unexpectedly Craig's eyes filled with tears but he went on, his voice even. "If he didn't have a strong will he'd probably be in a mental institution today. As it is, I think we're making progress with him; through hypnosis I've come very close to removing the block that keeps him mute. After tonight I suppose I'll have to start all over." He dried his eyes on the back of his hand and stood with his head bowed, staring down at the carpet. Outside, the bell tolled three times and Doremus cocked his head, listening.

"For what it's worth, I don't think Peter attacked me tonight," Doremus said. He raised his hand and gingerly touched the small bump on the back of his skull, near the right ear. "Someone else was in that mill with him." The Sheriff started to speak but Doremus cut him off. "I didn't see anyone else, Enoch, this is pure hunch. But I stand six-three and it's not likely Peter could have given me this whack on the head while he was on the run. And he was on the run all the time I was there, it was a game to him. I didn't hear him speak but I heard him giggling from excitement."

They were all looking at him now, except for Amy, who seemed to have turned to stone in front of the windows. "Peter was playing games tonight. He didn't go to the mill to kill me or anybody else. Even when he was stalking me with that lighted torch there was something odd about the way he acted. I believe he was only trying to hand me the torch, because that's what he'd been told to do. He was puzzled because I didn't want it." Doremus fell silent awhile, then he said sharply, "Does that make sense to you, Amy?"

She wasn't startled, but she turned and looked his way rather vaguely before replying. "Yes," she said then, her voice pitched low, "I'm beginning to see what all this means." Her eyes strayed momentarily to the window. "After all, he has been leaving here, sometimes late at night, we're sure of that, so something —someone is making him take such terrible chances. So it has to be. Peter is possessed. There is no other explanation." She looked defiantly at Craig, at the befuddled headmaster. "No other," Amy repeated, and her voice was brittle, her eyes wide and frightened. "Michael Young has control of him. He's making Peter do these awful things."

Thirteen

SHE DROVE A GOOD USED MUSTANG AND DROVE IT WELL, RUBBING her eyes and shrugging her shoulders from time to time to keep alert. Doremus slouched in the seat next to her and wished for a cigar. He said, "If it wouldn't be too much trouble I'd like to recover my motor scooter. Left it in some bushes down near the gristmill."

"No trouble," Amy said a trifle grimly.

They drove down Millican Dairy Road, raising dust, and

Amy slowed when the bridge over the creek came into her headlights.

"I meant to ask Craig if he saw anything when he came down this road tonight," Doremus said. "Slipped my mind."

"That was after all the excitement. Besides, he might have driven over by way of 22. Brunell's place is closer if you cut off the state road." They rattled across the loosely planked bridge. "Where do you want me to stop?"

"Anywhere beyond the bridge. Good thing Craig showed up when he did; we would have had a great deal of trouble getting Peter back to the school."

"Well, Craig has his eye on a gorgeous bronze nude about so high that Brunell got in two or three weeks ago. He's practically been living over at the gallery, trying to get Abe to come down on it a hundred or so." She turned off the engine. "I guess it would be better to put your scooter in the trunk rather than in the back seat. We can tie the lid down if need be."

Amy was wearing a ribbed pink turtleneck sweater, dark-green ski pants and black boots, so their trek between the thick brush on the slope and the flowing water was no hardship for her. Directly below the gristmill Doremus extended a hand and hauled her up the slippery bank. They stood close together in the moonlight, in silence, studying the entrance. The dirt of the clearing was completely tracked up.

"Where did you fall?" Amy asked, and he showed her. "That far? You might have been killed."

"After you fell into the pond they ran, didn't they? Both of them. He—Michael—must have thought you were dead."

Amy looked at Doremus, her eyes dark caves in the moonlight.

"He drives a car, of course; it's the only way he could get Peter back and forth. So his car was hidden somewhere off the road. Peter, meanwhile, was on the loose. What would you do, if you were Michael?"

"I'd . . . wait for him. Near the car."

"And then if Peter didn't make it back you'd have to go looking for him. Since you'd last seen him on the meadow you'd have to search there, but you couldn't risk being seen yourself. So you'd return to the woods, you'd go to the edge of the meadow and start walking, until you crossed the marsh and reached the Brunell place."

Amy nodded tautly. "Yes."

"And then you'd see Peter, up there on the hill, near the barn, the Brunell Gallery, and know you couldn't take the chance of calling him. You'd have to go and get him, lead him back to the car, then clear out." He walked with Amy to the moonlighted meadow, which was lightly frosted now. They left footprints in the stiffened grass.

"But that's where I went, searching for Peter," Doremus said. "To the Brunell place. Peter must have seen me coming, and . . . Michael undoubtedly saw me too, from the woods. He saw me and realized there was nothing he could do, realized he couldn't get to Peter before I did. So he returned through the woods to the place where he'd put his car. It must have been up the road aways, where the sound of an engine turning over would be muffled. And then he—"

"He drove away," Amy finished, too quickly.

Doremus turned off the light and faced her, and they stood ankle deep in the soft glowing meadow, his breath mildly steaming. Amy seemed to have stopped breathing, but her body was racked, she trembled from the cold and something more; there were tear tracks on her cheeks, like poured silver.

"I don't think so," Doremus said. "He drove only as far as the Brunell place. And it wasn't anybody named Michael."

"God," Amy's voice broke. "God, God, no, don't, stop, you hear, Doremus? I won't listen!"

"That was a good summation you made at the school, Amy. You put together what we knew, and what we suspected, and what we hoped was true, you put it all together beautifully and it sounded good. But it wasn't the whole truth, because the truth is even more frightening, more grotesque. We have to let it out though, Amy. We have to let the truth breathe."

"No, no, it couldn't be!"

"There's no Michael Young living in The Shades now, plotting and killing in memory of his dear mother. Michael Young *did* die in that blizzard, and his ghost rests. There is no Michael Young. He does not live. Despite all of Craig's sick efforts to bring him back to life in the person of Peter Mathis."

He was prepared for almost any reaction but violence. Amy launched herself at him, fists flailing, landing blows on his forehead, shoulders, chest. She hadn't the breath for screaming, but the sounds in her throat were worse than screaming. Doremus tried to tie up her arms and she butted him under the chin with her head, knocking him down. She came stomping

94

with her boots, like a man, breath rasping, the odd squealing noise rising and falling in her throat like the notes of an idiot's whistle. He decided she had to be fought as a man even as he was rolling out from under her boots. He blocked a kick at his throat, grabbed an ankle, twisted hard. Amy fell heavily but the crusty deep meadow grass softened the fall. She sat up determinedly, legs threshing, one clawlike hand raking toward his face. He pushed the hand aside and slapped her roughly. Amy's head whipped around and there was a startled gleam in one black eye, but her mouth was set in a savage line. Doremus belted her again and she dropped both arms and her head sank, blond hair spilling over the front of her sweater.

A cry of agony burst from Amy's throat. Her chest heaved. Even as he stood over her, ready to hit her again, Doremus could not help feeling a twinge of lust. He was grimly amused: it had been many months since he'd felt any sort of sexual desire at all. Then tenderness swept over him, and pity. He reached down, grasped an elbow, sought to lift her to her feet. She came halfway, eyes closed. Her throat muscles worked convulsively. Doremus let go and she turned around and threw up with as much violence as she had put into assaulting him.

He left Amy there and went down by the millrace, tore the shirt the sculptor had given him and returned to the meadow, where Amy now lay stretched out on her face. He kneeled beside her, turned her over, wiped her puffed face with the wet piece of shirt. She flinched and tried to pull away.

"I want to die," she groaned.

He took a deep breath and stood. She lay boneless in the crushed meadow, weakly gasping. He bent over and flicked the wet cloth across her face, stinging her.

"Get up," he said. "I'm not going to carry you. You're big enough to walk." When Amy didn't obey immediately he hit her again with the lash of the cloth. Her eyes popped open. She glared up at him. Even by moonlight he could see the reddening cheek, the thin welt. She put a hand to her injured cheek.

"You didn't have to do that!"

"On your feet."

Amy sat up, then with an effort made it to her feet. Doremus looked dispassionately at her. She said, in a voice thick with anger, "I think you're the most loathsome man I've met in my life. I mean it. I didn't like you from the first day I met you. You're arrogant and cold and boorish. I just wanted you to know that." She walked off briskly, down the slope of the meadow to the clearing in front of the mill. There she stopped, uncertainly, touched her cheek again, and began sobbing, swaying on her feet. She cried like an abused and misunderstood child.

"He must be . . . so terribly sick. I don't know why . . . I didn't see it sooner. All these months. So evasive, so preoccupied. How long was he carrying all that around in his mind? Oh, God, God, God, *what* can I do, how can I help him?"

"It's important to remember this, Amy. He is sick. And he's extremely dangerous. He's more dangerous at this moment than he's ever been, because he must realize we're getting close to him."

She pulled away, saying, in a horrified tone, "Peter!"

"Peter's safe with Craig; in fact Peter may be the only one who's safe with him just now."

"What about all he's made Peter go through in the past few weeks? Climbing over the roofs of the school . . . he could have been killed at any time. What has Peter had to do with Andy's death, and Hap's? Doremus, there's so much I don't understand!"

"And most of all, I don't understand why!" Amy cried.

"We've heard time and again about how much Michael loved his mother. We've heard how he rebelled against everybody when she died, retreated into himself, tried over and over to escape, to run away. But what do we know about Craig's reactions? How did he take his mother's death? Was he unaffected? I doubt it. I think he was as hurt and angered and resentful as his brother; but, emotionally, they weren't alike. Craig seems to have been the kind to button his lip, keep things to himself, never, never show his emotions. Besides, he had an extra burden, his little brother. He must have felt responsible for Mike because they were alone, in the care of an aunt whom they didn't know, whom they undoubtedly disliked and mistrusted at first. It was the world against the Youngs, and Craig felt bound to protect Michael at all costs. You can imagine how Michael's death hit him—when he failed in his trust."

Amy was sitting up now, her face stiff, listening. She moistened her lips with her tongue. "He must have felt . . . guilty. Intensely, morbidly guilty."

"I would say so. And as he grew older the pressure of that

guilt became too intense for him; it had to produce a few cracks in the psyche, give reality some odd twists. He had to be suffering. What happens to the individual who lives so long with guilt, keeping his emotions properly under control all the time?"

Amy was silent for a while, and then she said haltingly, "He can . . . destroy himself. Or he can shift the burden, make others carry part of it for him."

"Others, like Helen Connelly. Or Andrew Britton. Hap Washbrook."

"Doremus . . . what made you suspect it had to be Craig?"

"I began speculating when I saw how dependent on Craig Peter was. Also, an interesting thing happened in that barn while I was trying to corner Peter. I inadvertently started a bell tolling, and after it tolled ten, maybe a dozen times, Peter nearly jumped out of his skin, like a . . . a sleepwalker waking, and he seemed to have no awareness of where he was. The shock almost caused him a bad fall. Later, when I heard the bell at the Greenleaf School, which has a similar tone, it occurred to me that Peter might have been under hypnosis all the time I was chasing him—that he'd been cued to wake up, in his own room, at a certain hour, by the tollings of the school bell. By 'wake up' I mean from induced sleep. Then Craig mentioned he'd been using hypnosis as a part of Peter's therapy. I had already come up with the idea that Peter was getting out of his room at night by leaping like a tender young mountain goat over the rooftops of the school, and then I knew how it could be possible. He was doing it under deep hypnosis. Craig had been controlling almost every move Peter made until Peter blundered away from him tonight."

"Something like that occurred to me. If Peter was leaving the school at will, then someone had to be helping him. Someone who could drive in and out of the school grounds at all hours, without being challenged or remembered: a familiar face. When I made myself accept that I knew it all, because . . ." she hesitated, weakening, and leaned toward him again; Doremus held her, lightly, the crown of her head tucked under his chin. "Upstairs in the infirmary, while Peter was in a frenzy, Craig almost broke down. No. He did break down. I was in the outer room, the dispensary, trying to locate an ampul of meprobamate. The nurse is an old girl who can't see a foot without her glasses and Peter was upsetting her. Anyway, when I found the ampul I let her prepare the injection and went back to Craig. He was sitting on the bed holding Peter tightly in his arms and at first I thought there must be another boy with them, in the shadows somewhere, because I heard this voice saying, 'Don't, Michael . . . you're not lost, you're not lost . . .' This . . . little boy's voice. But the whole room was empty, only the three of us were there. It was Craig. And that voice . . . I'd heard it before. Just the other morning, on the telephone. Craig hadn't been gone from my bed thirty minutes when . . . *that* voice, that same voice. Said he was Michael. Said he hated Craig." She tensed in his arms; Doremus held her tighter. "Oh, God," she whimpered. "I'm so scared!"

Fourteen

HELEN WOKE UP AT SEVEN-THIRTY, EARLIER THAN PEGGY FOR once. Her daughter slept beside her, on her stomach, small hands, clutching the plump pillow.

It was a clear still cold morning. There was frost on the layer of yellow and ocher leaves in the backyard. Helen put on the best robe she had, the one that was pure extravagance, with yards of lace at the cuffs and down the front. She went downstairs, and was surprised to see the door of the office standing wide. She missed the morning effluvium of stale cigar smoke. She looked in. Apparently Doremus had come and gone, with all his belongings. The blankets and the pillow he had used were in the middle of the rusty-looking horsehair sofa. On top there was a scrawled note, the pale yellow rectangle of a telegram. She picked up the note.

Helen:
As you can see from the telegram I have to go up to Platteville for a while. Swen and his wife practically raised me, it's all I can do. I'll catch the seven a.m. bus to Ft. Wood, from there I can fly to St. Louis and on

to Dubuque, then drive the rest of the way. With luck I'll be back late tomorrow night. We had some excitement last night; Sheriff Mills will tell you about it if you give him a call.

Don't worry.

Doremus

Helen shook her head at the cryptic *Don't worry*. She read the note again, and glanced at the telegram. UNCLE SWEN SERIOUSLY ILL CAN YOU COME LOVE MEDA. She frowned and went out into the foyer, wondering if it was too early to call Enoch Mills. Then she decided she didn't care what time it was, and hastily dialed his home number.

The sun falling directly on the east window of her cubbyhole bedroom was like a candle flame held close to Amy's cheek. She stirred, coughed, awakened. Her eyes burned; she was not sure where she was until she saw the familiar flowered design of the spread piled up on the floor. She rolled over, her stomach lurching along a second later, falling into place like a stone. She had slept in soiled clothes, with a dirty face. She ached in a dozen vital places.

Amy staggered up and regarded herself in the sunlit vanity mirror. Her face was a patchy red, one cheek deeply creased by the ribbed sweater she wore. *Sunday*, she thought. *I look like I've been drunk. Played the part once. No good at it.*

Amy saw her mouth sag, fought the growing pressure of tears. She turned away quickly and stood, knees pressed together, in the middle of her sunny bedroom, toes in, trembling. She had lost all sense of direction; she cowered at the thought of the world waiting, as it waited every morning, to be approached with confidence, or to be feared. A large part of her confidence had been Craig. She had loved him, fought with him, cherished him, slept with him. How simple if he were dead, she thought. Then I could really mourn him, with honesty and a saddened heart. It would be easy to mourn, and gradually forget, and go on.

But he is not dead.

I'm not afraid of him, she told herself. *Yesterday I loved him— I know I loved him.* She tried, but could feel no sense of love, which shamed her. *I'm a psychologist, I understand these things. I can help him. Can't I help him?*

99

Amy knew what she must do, and she knew it was getting dangerously late.

Because it was Sunday she parked in the drive just behind the administration building. Craig's Chevelle was in front of her, forty feet away. She stared at it, looked away, stubbed out the cigarette she'd been smoking in the ashtray. She walked around the building to the shadowy wide steps and let herself in. As far as she could tell, the lower floor was deserted, filled with an amber light. She went first to her own office, making no noise. Inside she searched in her desk for the key to Craig's office, which he had given her long ago. She was hoping she wouldn't find it, but it was there with the rubber bands and the paper clips.

Craig's office was almost the length of the hall away. Amy knocked softly on the walnut-inlaid door and waited numbly, breathing through her mouth. She knocked again to make sure he wasn't there. Then she slipped the key into the lock, turned it, let herself in.

Amy went through the desk drawers first, finding them cluttered with tabbed folders, files of letters. It was slow work; she studied every note in Craig's hand for mention of Peter. At first she looked often at her wristwatch, worried about the minutes ticking away. She had no idea where Craig was. He could be upstairs in the infirmary close to Peter, perhaps sleeping in the next bed. Or he might be approaching his office right now. She glanced up, bit her lip sharply, went back to work.

The bottom drawer of the file contained a dozen boxes of tape for the compact Wollensak recorder on Craig's desk. Amy hunkered down, searched through the boxes. None were labeled. She considered taking them all, listening to them in the privacy of her own office. But she realized that would take hours, and if he returned to his office and happened to miss the tapes . . .

Amy stood and pushed the drawer in with the toe of one shoe, feeling defeated. Vacantly she gazed at the tape recorder. Apparently Craig had been using it recently. Amy considered the half-used spool of tape. Then, impulsively, she punched the proper buttons, rewound the tape, adjusted the tuning disc to a whisper and started the machine again. The tape unwound smoothly and silently. Amy looked at her watch again: a minute and a half had passed. There was nothing on the tape.

"I'll kill you sheriff I'll kill you I'll kill you I'll shoot you right in the goddam guts if you don't leave my mother alone—"

Amy stiffened, felt her heart contract painfully as the childish vituperation poured from the speaker.

"You're going to leave her alone you better not touch her you're going to learn to keep your damn hands off her You're going to stop f—"

Unthinkingly Amy reached down and turned the machine off with a stab of her finger. The skin of her face felt icy. She was torn between listening to all of it and running, running until she was out in the cool autumn afternoon, in the bright sun. She looked away, through the tilted-down blinds. There were a few boys in the quadrangle, moving slowly, gesturing. Tears came to her eyes.

She saw Craig then, on the walk in front of the cafeteria. Peter was with him, a step behind, looking serious and frail. Craig was smoking his pipe. They were walking toward the administration building. As she watched, Craig turned and said something to Peter. He seemed to smile. Shocked, Amy took a step back, although there was no chance that he could see her even if he happened to look directly at his windows. She could not help thinking how ordinary the scene was, Craig strolling on the Sunday campus with one of the boys. He was a favorite of a good many of them; she had seen him many times from her own windows, and felt a burst of pride.

The scathing, ten-year-old voice she had heard as the metallic brown tape unwound intruded on this memory. Amy moved quickly and soundlessly across the carpet, let herself out, remembered to lock the door behind her. She fled down the hall, entered her own office, threw herself down on the whooshing couch. She lay there for five minutes, for ten, motionless, hands over her face.

Amy realized now how Craig could have been at Helen's when Michael called. The voice had been on tape. Peter made the call from Craig's house, and activated the tape recorder.

If you need me, Doremus had said, *walk out on the quadrangle. Wear a pink sweater. I'll come on the run. It might take me ten minutes, twelve minutes . . . I don't know. But I'll get there.*

After a while Amy lifted her head, listening. She had heard the two of them when they entered the building, but there hadn't been a sound since. Possibly they had gone upstairs to the infirmary.

She glanced at the pink sweater folded over the back of the chair behind her desk. Then she left the office without taking the sweater, walked nervelessly down the long hall. There were glimmerings of sun on the brown tile floor. She carried the key to Craig's office in one sweaty fist.

Craig had turned on the desk lamp and closed the blinds all the way. He sat behind the desk, his chair tipped back against the windowsill. There was a vertical line of strain between his eyes, but his voice was low, controlled. Peter sat nearby, in a high-backed wing chair, his feet on an ottoman. His head was tilted to one side and his eyes were closed. He had gone very easily into deep hypnotic sleep, in a matter of seconds. He had a curious, lifeless look, his skin waxen against the deep red of the leather chair.

"Your mother is there, Peter," Craig said, his eyes on the child's still face. "She's in the room with you. And you're happy to see her. Very happy. You're close to her. You love her very much."

Peter's eyelids fluttered, and his throat muscles worked. Gradually a smile appeared, but he lost his hold on it. He trembled, lightly, in his sleep. Craig leaned forward, worriedly.

"It's all right, Peter. You're with your mother, and everything is all right. You're going to speak to her today. You want very much to speak to her, to . . . tell her that you love her." Craig's voice weakened. "We only have . . . a little more time, Peter. Today you have to speak to her."

Outside, the wind had risen, driving leaves against the windows. Craig looked up distractedly, then returned his attention to Peter.

"Please try. Please speak to me."

The boy's back arched as if he were in pain. He fell back, groaning. But he said nothing.

Craig continued to watch Peter's face, intently and hopefully. Then his own throat muscles tightened. He rubbed his eyes remorsefully.

"You're not *trying*," he said brokenly. "Peter, you're . . ." The wind sighed, vibrating the glass of the windows. "Let's go back once more, to . . . to . . ." His mouth turned down petulantly. For a few moments there was sharp hatred in Craig's eyes. He reached suddenly, savagely, for Peter. The wind moaned, stopped him. Craig stepped back in fright. There was a roaring in his mind; the wind had become a bitter gale. He felt the barrenness of perpetual winter in his heart. His knees gave way and he slipped down beside the chair. In the horrid winter wastes of his heart a stricken eleven-year-old boy lived again. The cry from his heart was a cry of endless terror, or loss.

Michaeellll

"Michael," Craig said, writhing on the carpet. "Come back!"

He began crawling, slowly and torturously, sobbing in his throat. A few feet from the chair he toppled. His feet threshed against the carpet. Each violent breath knotted him. He was as speechless as Peter Mathis, who slept obliviously in the chair a few feet away. But, gradually, recognizable words were wrenched from his throat—adolescent, rambling phrases became clear, spoken in a high, youthful voice.

"Look what Mike made for you, Mother. I helped him. We went down to the creek today; you ought to see how full it is! There was a big black snake in a tree. Mike swam right under it and didn't see it. I held my breath under water a minute and a half. Mike counted . . ."

Before long he lay quietly on the soft carpet in the darkened room. Occasionally his chest heaved. He was quiet, but tension has scored his face. Then, abruptly, he sat up, listening, eyes alert. The sleeping boy attracted him. He walked over to the chair, looking grave and studious. When he spoke again his phrasing was that of an adult, but it was the same clear, childish voice.

"I know why you won't talk to me. I understand, Mike. I *let* them take Mother away." Craig's face darkened with resentment and hatred but he went on. "I found you, though. That's the important thing. We all thought you were gone, but I found you. You *will* speak to me again, won't you, Mike? Tonight. After the last one is dead."

He sat down behind the desk, a very purposeful eleven-year-old boy. "I saved her for last. I know you want to help me tonight, Michael. I know you want to help me kill her. Auntie Helen *hated* Mother. She really deserves to die. More than the others. She's going to get what's coming to her." He was silent, thinking. "We'll call her on the phone again. I'll say . . ." His voice went even higher, and his eyes widened in excitement. "Auntie Helen, this is Michael! I have to see you; a terrible thing is going to happen to Craig! Please come, I'm at Craig's house—please hurry.' " Craig shot a look at the sleeping boy, pleased with himself, and he giggled suddenly, covering his mouth with one hand. Then he reached out and turned on the tape recorder.

"*. . . king my mother, you're not ever going to get near her again you're not—*"

Craig hastily punched the button that stopped the tape; he sat stiffly for three or four seconds, staring at the machine. Fury reddened his eyes and he leaped from the chair in which he'd been sitting. The chair banged against the windowsill. Peter twitched in his sleep but his eyes remained closed. Craig raced for the office door, opened it.

The hallway outside was clear.

Craig made a savage sucking noise in his throat. For a few moments he felt dizzy. He leaned against the jamb, staring down the deserted hall. Midway there was a hot blaze of light: the westerly sun was shining through the glass of the entrance doors. The harsh light made Craig's eyes water. But he noticed something else at the far end of the hall, another vivid stripe of sun slashed diagonally across the dull brown tile. Almost as soon as he became aware of the stripe it vanished. A door had been quietly closed.

Something like a smile appeared on Craig's face, but his jaw muscles were rigid. He pulled the door of his office shut and began walking. Opposite the entrance he shielded his eyes from the glaring afternoon sun. Only a little of the fury had left his eyes. It made the clamped, jaw-breaking smile uniquely terrible.

When he reached Amy's office he didn't hesitate but yanked open the door and stepped inside. Amy was standing by her desk, visibly out of breath. Her head jerked around at his coming. She jumped half a foot.

Craig said, in his own voice, "You have a key to my office. I want it."

His eyes fumed, brooded. He stood slightly hunched, wolflike: he was totally unfamiliar. Amy tried to find something in him to respond to. She could do nothing but shake her head in weak protest.

Craig's smile faded. He moved closer, looking her over. Amy's right hand was clenched on the desk top.

He said offhandedly, "You're a no-good goddamned whore. You know that, don't you?"

Amy's breath hissed. She had been prepared for anything but indignity, humiliation. The slap of it gave her new life, a flickering of courage. "Why? Why am I that?" Her eyes were steady on him; tears formed in them. "Because I . . . loved you?"

"Give me the key or I'll break your hand."

Amy turned her hand over and the key rang on the glass surface of the desk. "Here. Take your key. Craig, I want . . . I want very much to talk to you. Will you sit down?"

Craig's eyes darted to the key. His smile came and went. He reached for the key. She wasn't watching; she was still looking at his face. His hand paused above the key, then closed on a baseball-size glass paperweight with a gorgeous orange-and-black butterfly inside.

Amy touched his left-hand sleeve, imploringly. "Craig, it's so important that we—"

He hit her, somewhat awkwardly, over the left ear with the heavy paperweight. Amy made a meaningless sound in her throat and buckled. As she went down her hands tightened on his jacket. Her eyes opened partway and she looked up at him, dazed.

Craig was bent by the strength of her hands. "I don't *want* to talk to you," he said earnestly, his voice high. He swung the paperweight again, from above his head. In the golden dusty silence of the little office the paperweight made a brutal rapping sound on the flat of Amy's skull. She slid limply to the floor. There was a red seeping at the roots of her blond hair.

Craig looked at her for perhaps half a minute. He set the paperweight aside, picked Amy up in his arms, grunted, threw her down again on the carpet behind her desk. He stood back, near the door. One of her legs from the knee down was visible protruding from behind the desk. He returned and bent the leg at the knee until it was hidden. He looked once more at her dry white face, bluish around the eyes, hollow in the temples. He had hit her very hard and he didn't know if she was breathing or not. He had no desire to find out.

He let himself out of the office and walked slowly down the hall, shambling a little, not picking up his feet.

Peter was in the same position in the wine-red high-backed chair, his small-boned hands slack in his lap. Craig squatted beside the chair, he ran his hand lightly, sympathetically over the head of the sleeper. Peter sighed, fitfully.

"I'm sorry, Michael," Craig whispered. "I'm sorry you have to go out tonight. But it's necessary."

Fifteen

DOREMUS HAD CHOSEN A PLACE ON THE RAZORBACK, ALMOST directly above the school. There had been a minor rock slide in the area a year ago, clearing brush and loose soil, so nothing interfered with his line of sight. He sat with his back against an old elm tree with half its roots exposed where the slide had pared the declivity to clean rock.

Hourly he arose and pulled himself up to level ground and walked around to get the kinks out of his knees and loosen stiffened muscles, then clambered down to resume his wait. He had a pair of 7x50 Japanese-made binoculars around his neck. His cache included a stock of cigars and a quart canteen of water. He also had a compact Citizens' Band radio along; he had used it twice, the first time around noon when he observed Amy Lawlor's car entering the school grounds. The second time had been at sundown, and he'd had nothing of interest to report.

The faint steady hum of the CB radio was interrupted by Enoch Mills' voice.

"Doremus?"

He reached down and picked up the radio microphone. "Right here."

"I make it ten after nine. Anything stirring?"

"No. Peter and Craig apparently had dinner in Craig's office . . . I saw a tray being carried over. Then Peter left the administration building, alone, at seven, and walked across the quadrangle to his hall. I suppose he's in bed. The lights in Dobbs went out on schedule, and Franklin Hall should go dark in five minutes. As far as I know, Craig is still in his office."

"What about the girl? She was only going to be there an hour at the most."

Doremus hesitated; he had thought about little else during the past few hours. "I don't know where she is. I've had the glasses on her office window but I can't tell a thing. There aren't any lights."

"She must have run into trouble then. I think we ought to move in."

"If she's in trouble, that might make it worse. And if she's . . . dead, then we're too late already. I have a feeling something's about to happen, otherwise Craig would have gone home by now. Let's give him a little more time."

Tree shadows danced in the circles of light on the quadrangle. He turned the glasses on the dark bulk of the residence halls. He could not see the inner windows but the slant of the roof shone in the moonlight, gun-metal gray. He traced the roof line, focused for a few moments on the black half-acre of parking lot, the delivery area and loading dock behind the cafeteria. There was a stabbing pain in his left shoulder he hadn't been able to work out. He ignored it, returned his attention to the roof of Dobbs Hall.

The boy had appeared there as if conjured. He stood, motionless, straight, assured, in the moonlight. Doremus felt his throat squeezing tight. For several seconds Peter seemed to be listening, to be looking for something. A gust of wind almost unbalanced him. He recovered, then began running, nimbly, across the tar-and-gravel surface. Doremus tracked him, marveling. When he reached the limit of the roof Peter leaned momentarily over the parapet, looking down at the vertical mat of ivy on the otherwise blank wall.

"Watch yourself, kid," Doremus said under his breath. "Maybe you've done it before, but take care."

Confidently the boy climbed over the two-foot-high parapet, held on with both hands while he dug with his toes into the tough vine. Doremus couldn't tell if he was wearing sneakers. When he seemed sure of a foothold Peter started down. It was difficult to follow his progress, even with the good binoculars, because of the dark background. It seemed to take him the better part of five minutes to go just a few feet .

Quite suddenly, as Doremus watched edgily, Peter appeared to lose his grip, or perhaps the vine pulled away from the wall. He was free of the wall, falling. Doremus leaned forward, helplessly. Peter landed on his feet on the covered walkway to the cafeteria, swayed there, took a hasty step to steady himself.

It looked as if he would fall again, headfirst to the asphalt parking strip. But he regained balance and went down on one knee to catch his breath.

The rest of the way down was easy for him: an eight-foot jump to the grassy terrace. He picked himself up, vanished beneath the walkway. Doremus tried vainly for a couple of minutes to pick him up again. When he had his next glimpse of Peter, the boy was running at the edge of the drive, circling behind the administration building. Doremus turned the binoculars on the Chevelle. Craig was standing beside it, waiting.

He spoke to Peter, briefly, dropping a hand on his shoulder. Then he opened a door of the car and Peter got in. Instead of getting into the car himself, Craig walked briskly back to the building.

Automatically Doremus looked at the glowing face of his chronometer: nine minutes past ten. He raised the binoculars again.

At twenty after, Craig reappeared, carrying Amy.

The distance was too great for Doremus to tell what condition she was in, or if she was bound. Craig held her with one arm while he lifted the lid of the trunk. Unhappily there was no revealing flash of light from inside the trunk. But judging from the loose way she sprawled when Craig put her inside, she was at least unconscious, if not dead. The hatred he felt for Craig Young was as blinding as a migraine headache. He reached down, groped for the CB radio, put it in his lap. He kept his eyes on the Chevelle while he brought Enoch Mills in.

"We've got some action. Also complications. Craig's about to leave the school. Peter Mathis is in the back seat of the car, probably lying flat so he won't be seen when Craig drives through the gate. And Amy is in the trunk."

"What shape is she in?"

"I don't know. Half an hour closed up in that trunk and she's a goner no matter what. OK, he's just leaving the grounds. Better have the boys in the other car close slow. No light. He may be panicky."

"We're ready for him," Enoch said crisply. "Come a runnin'."

Doremus clutched the radio in one hand and pulled himself up the slope. When he was standing, he unclipped the flashlight from his belt and cut his way through the buckbrush with it. Twenty yards away was an old logging road, a barely passable slash up the wooded spine of the razorback. He would never have gotten a car up there and in fact he'd had to push his scooter part of the way, but he anticipated only moderate difficulty going down. He stowed the radio away, fixed the lamp to the handlebars for additional light, kicked the motor to life and went charging away, head low to avoid the unexpected lash of a low-hanging limb.

If he's driving slow, Doremus thought, plummeting toward the valley on the atrocious road, his no longer young bones taking a pounding, *if he's driving slow and watching the bad curves in that road and maybe talking to Peter, then I've got a one-minute lead on him. Time to ditch the scooter and dig in by the side of the road with the Woodsman. Just in case it takes three men.* But he wasn't planning to mix in. It was up to Mills now. Craig probably wouldn't recognize the under sheriff right away, not without his uniform.

That girl, he thought. *I don't believe I could forgive myself if* —He brought the scooter to a skidding stop, parked it, ran for the blacktop road, pulling the Colt from his waistband. He saw the sheriff's car just before the big curve, taillights glowing. The deputy was under the hood with a flashlight. He had a sawed-off shotgun in his other hand. Mills leaned against the side of his car, a big white Pontiac. The beam of his flashlight circled lazily on the road. He turned his head as Doremus approached, gasping for breath.

"Likely spot there," he said, pointing. "Good cover; he won't pick you up in his headlights."

"As soon as you pull him out of the car I'll go for the boy."

"Fine idea."

"How far behind him are your boys?"

"Reckon about a thousand yards. He won't know they're there, but if he tries to back off on us they'll block him right quick."

"Well, he's due," Doremus said. Except for the toneless wind moan, the night was still. Early frost had driven cicadas and tree frogs into the mud, and they were not close to farms or houses and the inevitable dogs. Doremus went down on his elbows below the road.

Three more minutes passed. Mills shuffled his feet on the asphalt and spat. The deputy said hoarsely, "Where's he at?"

"Maybe he had a flat tire," Mills said. "Hold it!"

Doremus looked up. A squad car came slowly into view, lights out.

"Be damned," Mills said sullenly, and wagged his flashlight. The squad car speeded up and jerked to a stop near him. Doremus got slowly to his feet. The deputy driving the squad car stuck his head out the window and said:

"Thought you'd have him. Where'd he go?"

"You tell me."

Doremus said, "You didn't pass him on the road?"

"Hell, no."

"Where could he have pulled off?" Doremus asked Mills.

"I don't know. Chuck, bring me the map."

The other two deputies remained in the squad car with the engine idling. The driver switched on his headlights as Mills unfolded the big Geological Survey map of Shades County on the trunk of his Pontiac.

"Here's the only access road between this point and the school," he muttered, aiming his flashlight at one grid of the map. "It's dirt, winds down across Settler Creek and through this bottom land, past a good-size gravel pit. Comes out a quarter mile from the Big Diamond truck stop on 60."

"Then he's on that road."

"Something made him nervous. Or maybe he meant to all the time. He might be looking for a place to—" Mills glanced up at Doremus with a hint of shock in his green eyes.

"To drop a body off," Doremus said, finishing it for him.

"That gravel pit would be ideal," Mills admitted. "But there's other places he could do it, and she might not be found for a while." The map bellied as the wind blew hard and Mills had to hold it down with both hands.

"It's also possible he pulled off behind the barricade and stopped there with his lights off," Doremus speculated. "Because . . . say he needed a couple of minutes to think something over. Maybe Amy is alive after all, and she was making noises in the trunk. Or he could have left something he needs at the school. If he was on the dirt road then he'd have seen the squad car go by with all lights out and become damned suspicious. That might have prompted him to double back this way." Doremus traced the Eveningshade Hollow road east, past the school and around the other end of the razorback. "If he did that, then he has a choice of roads by now. He could be anywhere."

Mills walked back to the squad car and spoke briefly to his boys. The driver turned the car around and they went off with a quick screech of tires.

"Told Bryant and McLemore to look for him this side of the bridge," Mills explained when he returned, "and I said if they was to see him then they should take him. If he ain't on the dirt road they'll make a circuit of the school grounds. Then they'll cruise all the roads between Constable Ridge and Blounstown."

"I'm wondering what Craig did to Amy. Did he make her tell that he was being watched? His actions so far indicate both carelessness and deep suspicion. What's going on in his mind? So far we've more or less assumed that he's rational, we've been trying to guess what a sane man with a body on his hands might do. But suppose he's broken down completely. He might have forgotten Amy's back there in the trunk. He might be driving around in the moonlight talking to himself with spit on his chin. And while we go off in all directions he's gradually working his way around to another victim: Helen."

"I could sure use some more men," Mills said with a sigh. "What the hell do we do? Stake out the Connelly house?"

"Not just yet. I imagine we've got an hour or two before Craig gets to Helen. In the meantime I think you ought to keep Bryant and the other deputy cruising. Who knows, they might find Craig pulled off by the side of the road somewhere reciting nursery rhymes. You might come across him sitting at the edge of the gravel pit counting bubbles where Amy sank." His forehead was deeply ridged. "I think we ought to spread out but be prepared to close quickly when Craig gives notice. I'm going to ride my scooter into the village. Helen was planning to take Peggy and me to the movies tonight—before I was called out of town, that is—and I might find them at the theater. Unfortunately it's time to bring her up to date on nephew Craig."

In the village he found the theater dark; the evening show had let out at ten. For that matter the downtown area was nearly deserted, with only two places of business open. They were both taprooms, one at each end of the main street.

There was a phone booth at the Gulf station two blocks north of the courthouse, so he got back on his scooter and went popping around the corner. By his chronometer it was ten minutes of eleven. Exactly half an hour since Craig had put

Amy in the trunk of his car. In Doremus' mind there was a vivid chilling image: Craig aimlessly driving and driving on the back roads of Shades County, driving long past the moment when Amy would take the last breath of foul trunk air and die. He discovered he was shaking, his bones ached. He gritted his teeth and parked the scooter next to the lighted phone booth and dialed Helen Connelly's number.

After he'd listened to a dozen rings he began sweating coldly. On the eighteenth ring Peggy answered, yawning at the same time. "H'lo."

"Peggy, this is Doremus."

"It is?" she said doubtfully.

"Yes. I'm back in The Shades now. Could I talk to your mother, please?"

"OK," Peggy said, and Doremus heard the receiver bump as she put it down on the table. "*Mo-ther! Doremus wants to talk to you!*"

Doremus leaned against one side of the booth, his eyes watering from strain. He fumbled in his shirt pocket for his Polaroid sunglasses and put them on. Two minutes passed; he couldn't hear Peggy anymore. Fear struck at the back of his neck, spread a swift paralysis down his spine.

"Peggy," he shouted into the receiver. "Peggy, do you hear me?"

Rigidly he waited another half minute; then, with a shock of relief, he heard her on the other end of the wire.

"I don't think she's here," Peggy said, uncertainly.

"Go to the door," he said, trying to keep his voice from betraying anxiety. "Look out and see if your mother's wagon is parked by the street."

"I can see from here," Peggy said. "It's gone. Where did Mother go, Doremus?"

"I . . . I don't think she went very far. Look, honey, do me a favor right now. I want you to go into the office as soon as you hang up and lock the door behind you. Make sure you lock the door, now. Wait there. Wait until Sheriff Mills comes. He'll be there in just a few minutes, and he'll call to you loud enough for you to hear. But don't . . . don't let anybody else in the house. Do you understand? Not even Craig. Stay in the office with the door locked. Even if you hear Craig calling you, don't go out."

"Why?"

"It's important, Peg. I'll explain later, when I see you.

That'll be soon. In the meantime, promise me you'll wait in the office for the sheriff?"

"Yes," Peggy said, as if she thought it was all rather silly. "Goodbye."

As soon as he had hung up Doremus retrieved the CB radio from his Cushman. "Mills!"

"This is Mills. What's up?"

"Where are you now?"

"Headed south on 22. We'll be at the gravel pit in about another four minutes."

"Can you turn around and get over to the Connellys'? I just talked to Peggy. She's alone there. Apparently Helen left her sleeping in her room and went off in a hurry somewhere; the ranch wagon is gone."

"Turn us around, Chuck," the sheriff said in an aside to his deputy. To Doremus he said, "Where do you suppose she went?"

"I don't know. She must have been convinced it was urgent; otherwise she wouldn't have left Peggy like that—particularly after I warned her. I think Craig got her out of the house."

"You suppose he's after the kid instead of Helen?" Dimly Doremus heard the screeching of tires as the deputy made a looping turn.

"He might be. I told Peggy to lock herself into the first-floor office and not open up for anybody but you. Holler loud when you hit the front porch."

"We can pick you up at 22 and White Church."

"No, I'm going to try to track Helen down."

"On that scooter? Let me get Bryant and McLemore over to you. Where you calling from?"

Doremus rubbed his forehead in agitation. "I've had a lot of sour hunches in the last three-quarters of an hour. I'd made up my mind that Craig was just driving around in a daze. I don't believe it now. He knows exactly what he's doing; he's working according to a timetable and so far everything's clicking nicely for him. Here's the last of my hunches, and God help the Connellys if I'm wrong. Craig isn't interested in Peggy, it's Helen he wants. He's lured her to a dark and private place where he plans to kill her."

"What place?"

"Two choices. He's had a fondness for the burned-out house where he and his brother lived; he's taken Peter there before.

According to his logic it might be the ideal setting to complete his cycle of revenge. It would take me half an hour to get there on my scooter though. Bryant and McLemore can make it in half the time."

"I'll contact them. Where are you headed?"

"Up Ben Lomond. Craig might have done the most predictable thing of all—driven straight home and called Helen from there. I know approximately where his house is, what it looks like. I can get up there in ten minutes."

"We'll be right behind you," Mills promised.

"Let me try it alone. He may be watching for a car and before you could get close he'd kill her, if he hasn't already. But a man on a motor scooter without lights isn't that easy to see, and he'll never hear me in this wind. Give me . . . half an hour. I think I can surprise him."

Craig had been living for the better part of two years in a house he rented from a man named Dillbeck, who had been both a governor and a United States senator until an upset victory by a well-heeled Republican had retired him from public office at the age of fifty-five. He had scarcely moved into his retirement house, which had taken months to build, when he was offered a choice assignment as an ambassador at large by his old buddy the President. Consequently he hadn't set foot in the state for over a year.

Helen drove haltingly through the gates and into the parking area, unnerved as always by the drive up, unnerved by the telephone call, the Michael call that had prompted her to grab her purse and coat and run from the house unthinkingly. She wondered now why she hadn't tried to contact the sheriff first—but there hadn't seemed to be any time at all. She had been afraid for Craig's life.

His car was there, facing the road. She pulled up behind it, got out. The wind tore at her hair, deafened her. She took three unsteady steps toward the house, head down. She didn't realize she had left the headlights of the car turned on.

The wind slowed; almost beside her she heard a childish giggling and she turned her head sharply.

A boy in cowboy clothes was standing there; big red Stetson-type hat tied under his chin, an imitation-leather vest with a shiny star pinned to it, imitation-fur chaps. He was pointing a silvery revolver at her.

He giggled again, and snapped off three rapid shots from the cap pistol. Helen nearly fell off the rock path to the iron stairs below. When she recovered he was gone: he had jumped nimbly from the ledge to a terrace of the garden. She could not find him in the tossing shadows. And then she had a glimpse of his red hat as he peered out at her from behind a square-trimmed shrub.

"Come here," she made herself say. "I want you to . . . Who are you?" She knew who it must be, but she couldn't think of a name. Not Michael though. Certainly not Michael. Her relief was distinct, warming. This was a real boy, playing a boy's game, he was not Michael.

But Michael had called her.

Helen started down to the first level of the garden, began walking to her left, toward the place where she had seen him. She was holding her hands to her ears, trying to shut out the incessant wind. She saw him again.

Popping up one level down, from the shadows of a plumelike waving tree that grew twenty feet tall.

"Come here . . . please come here! I want to talk to you! Where's Craig?" She stopped and looked hopefully at the house. But it was completely dark. *Why?* she wondered. A hard wave of fear almost toppled her.

"Boy," she shouted, and his name came to her tongue. "Peter! Quit playing now. I have to talk to you."

There was a lull; she heard the popping of the cap gun. Turning quickly, she saw him run from one place of concealment to another.

Helen followed. She was in the midst of the garden now, surrounded by all the carefully nurtured oddities foreign to the soil of Missouri. Above the wind a few stars glimmered undisturbed. She went on, searching carefully.

Out of the tail of her eyes she saw something moving on the gallery of the house. Helen stared, trying to make out what it was. . . . A dog? But a dog wouldn't move so awkwardly. She was drawn closer to the gallery. Behind her the little boy giggled; she was absorbed and horrified by the creeping shape on the gallery and didn't bother to turn around.

"Craig?" Helen said, once again. The thing stopped. Helen walked to within a few feet of the gallery, but she still couldn't see what it was. Then she realized that it must be Craig, on all fours.

He's hurt, and started for the stairs.

Behind her there was a throaty, drawn-out shriek. The sound he was making numbed her as thoroughly as an electric shock. It seemed to take all of a minute for her to look around, to look up at him.

He was standing, fully visible against the dark-gray and star-shot sky. Helen saw that he wore almost no clothes, but nothing else could really surprise her because he was still shrieking. Her tongue felt bolted to the roof of her mouth and her heart was like a tight sack of broken glass. Vaguely she recognized the fierce and terrifying cries. She had heard them in a good many western movies just before the Indians swooped down and slaughtered all of the homesteaders. Unconsciously her mouth curled in an expression very like a smile, but she felt no laughter.

With ceremonial slowness Craig raised his right hand, raised it high. He was holding a thick-bladed knife almost ten inches long.

He came down then, with a step and a leap and another whoop, and crouched within five feet of her. She saw, more or less clearly, the dark stripings of paint on his naked chest and face. Her vision blurred momentarily, and then she focused on the hunting knife. As astounded as she was, Helen felt a definite fearful shriveling inside.

Enough, she wanted to say. *Don't anymore. Stop now. It isn't funny anymore*. And even as she was thinking this she realized with a horrid certainty that it wasn't a joke. He was going to kill her.

Doremus had come through the gates in a boil of black smoke and seen Helen's car, with headlights blazing, parked behind the Chevelle. His ears throbbed from the howl of wind and the racket of the failing scooter engine. He pulled up beside Craig's car, put the kick stand down with his foot and went for the trunk of the Chevelle. It wasn't locked.

Amy lay cramped inside, jackknifed, her back to him. There were streaks that could have been blood or grease in her blond hair. He found it difficult to free her because he was afraid to exert much force. He got one hand under a shoulder and another under her thighs and tugged gently, then turned her and lifted her out. Amy's head fell back and he looked at her besmirched, oddly flat-looking face. He could not tell if she had

116

suffocated there in the trunk. Her skin was cool to the touch.

He heard Helen scream, somewhere.

Doremus took two quick steps, wrenched open one of the doors of the Chevelle and laid Amy inside on the seat, face up. He closed the door, stepped back, drew the Colt automatic from his waistband and looked the house over. At first he couldn't see a way in. He heard Helen screaming again and then a series of flat cracking sounds, like undernourished firecrackers, or . . .

Cap pistol? he thought, and ran toward the fence. When he was on top of it he saw the outline of the door.

There seemed to be no one in the garden, but as he tried to orient himself the wind let up and the trees fell to quaking lightly; shadows froze. Then he could see them all, Peter in his cowboy suit and Craig—apparently—in his birthday suit. They were at the bottom of the sheltered garden, close to a low retaining wall of rock. Helen had fallen and she was trying to rise from her knees. She sobbed hysterically. Craig stood two or three feet behind her, hands at his sides: Doremus thought he heard a high-pitched and excited child's voice. Peter was farther away, on a tier above them, cap pistol in hand.

As Doremus watched, the knife in Craig's hand flashed up and he bent over his Aunt Helen. She looked back, screamed again. Instinctively Doremus raised his Colt, sighting. Then two things happened, quickly, confusingly. The wind tugged at his outstretched hand, spoiling his aim, and Peter, who had been motionless and absorbed, moved into the line of fire.

Doremus screamed, "Get out of there! Peter, move!"

Even as he said it Peter hurtled from the tier he had been standing on and landed, like a trained monkey, on Craig's back. Craig was staggered, but the knife slashed down and Helen pitched forward on her face. From where he was standing Doremus could not see if Craig had hit her with the blade. He began to run, recklessly, down the shallow garden steps.

"Mike," Craig said, in his childish voice, "get off, Mike! Let me finish!" He lunged to his feet, brushing the boy off his back; he made a quick move with his knife hand in the direction of the prostrate woman. But just as quickly Peter grabbed him around the legs, held him back. Craig tried to kick free. Peter was sobbing.

"Don't!" Peter said. "Don't hurt! Don't don't don't."

Craig lifted his head and saw Doremus coming. With a violent kick he sent Peter flying against the rock wall and dashed in the direction of the house. As soon as Craig detached himself from Peter, Doremus risked a shot, snapping it, but Craig was quick and the bullet went behind him.

Doremus continued on to the bottom of the garden and the paved walk there, knelt beside Helen. She was unconscious. He lifted her by one shoulder, saw the dark oozing wound, high, two or three inches from the base of her neck. Peter sat rubbing his head slowly, in a dazed way.

"From now on you're the sheriff," Doremus said to him, handing over the cap pistol Peter had dropped. He looked up and saw Craig midway on the gallery, running hard, bent over. Doremus lifted the Colt, led him, squeezed off a shot that nicked concrete ahead of the nearly naked man. He put another one into the redwood fence an instant after Craig opened the high door and excaped.

Doremus followed, missed a step, fell hard on the rough stone, tearing the knee out of his hunting pants, lacerating the palm of one hand. He scrambled up, unnecessarily furious with himself for having missed two chancy shots with an unfamiliar hand-gun. He tried running but had to adjust to a fast limping walk.

When he was still ten feet from the fence he heard the engine of the Chevelle turn over, roar loudly, heard the tires laying down rubber as Craig gunned away with the brakes on. Doremus wondered bleakly what he had been thinking about, putting Amy in that car. It had seemed like a good idea, but he should have taken the trouble to pull the keys from the ignition first.

The Chevelle tires were still peeling on the blacktop when another set of tires yelped and the night split open as two cars collided, ripping each other fender to fender. Doremus reached the open door in the gate as Enoch Mills' car came lurching into view, one headlight glaring angrily. They had met at the drive-way gates, where there was room for only a car and a half. Craig's Chevelle had veered several feet to the right, knocked down one of the brick posts and torn up several feet of valuable fencing before coming to a complete stop. For a few moments, in the wind lull, there was no sound but the hiss of escaping steam from the radiator of the sheriff's car; then the mashed door on the driver's side opened with a deadly grinding noise and the deputy named Chuck stepped out uncertainly, clutching his left arm below the elbow. He took two weaving steps, dropped to his knees, rolled slowly over, one cheek resting on the cold asphalt.

Doremus limped to the other side of the wrecked Pontiac, opened the door. Enoch Mills had pulled himself off the padded dash. There was a trace of blood on his mouth, and his lower lip appeared to be split. He shook his head a couple of times, sorrowfully, looked at Doremus.

"We come a little early," he explained.

Doremus helped him out. "I'm all right," Mills said. "What happened to Chuck?"

"Passed out." They both started around the car toward the fallen deputy. Doremus saw the smoke around the Chevelle then. He took a step in the direction of the other car, hesitated. Craig Young stumbled out of the hovering gray smoke, came straight at them. For a few moments the red streaks of paint on his face hid the fact that he was bleeding from the left temple. But he had held on to his knife somehow.

Doremus centered the muzzle of his automatic on Craig's heaving chest. "Throw it down," he said softly.

Craig stopped abruptly, looked at the two men with suspicion. He raised the knife a couple of inches, threateningly. Doremus calmly thumbed back the hammer of the Colt.

"What the hell," Mills said, staring. "Where's his clothes?"

"Brave warriors don't wear clothes. Right, Craig? Oh, your Aunt Helen's OK. You only got her in the shoulder. Now let's put the knife down and play some other game for a while; this one's been a little hard on everybody."

Blood dripped from Craig's left cheekbone. His lips parted and he showed his teeth. Doremus noted that he had shaved off the manly moustache. Without it his face looked thinner, flayed to the bone. Doremus could almost see Craig's heart beating through the ridged wall of his chest. The blood seemed to be flowing more profusely from the wound at his temple. Doremus felt a tug of pity for him, wondering at the same time if Sheriff Washbrook had seen something like this just before he was killed.

"One more time, Craig. The knife." He had the unhappy feeling that he was going to be forced to kill Craig, and he was already planning how to do it with a minimum of distress. At that range he knew he could not miss the heart, and Craig would be dead in the blink of an eye. But weariness befuddled him; for a couple of seconds the barrel of the automatic dipped.

Craig jumped at them, screaming, and hurled his knife. It hit Enoch Mills butt first over the left eye and he went over backward as if he'd been slugged. Instead of following the knife and charging, Craig whirled and made for the limestone cliff across the drive. Doremus aimed the automatic reluctantly. Then, as Craig began climbing, he put the Colt away and helped Mills to his feet.

"Where's he going?" Mills said, fingering the sore spot on his forehead.

"I don't think he knows. Up. Out, maybe. But he won't make it."

They watched silently as Craig continued to climb, frantically. They could hear him grunting, scrabbling with his fingernails. Small rocks rained on the blacktop. He was thirty feet up, looking pale and fragile against the cliff, when he began to falter. He pressed in, gripping the rock with every inch of his skinny body. The wind was troubling him. They heard him cry out, unintelligibly. Then he went on.

"I don't know if I can watch it," Mills muttered. He hauled Chuck off the paving, carried him to the Pontiac, which was tilted over a flattened tire, and put him in. Then he took his CB radio off the floor, tested it. Doremus stayed where he was, looking up. It was harder to see Craig now, but he could still be heard; each agonized breath cut through the dull sweep of the wind.

And then he came down in a shower of soft broken rock, came down like a featherless bird, arms outflung, still reaching for the last handhold. He hit the asphalt drive feet first, at a slight angle, collapsed, his head bouncing as it struck an instant later. He lay still and foreshortened and the stripes of red war paint gleamed in the light from the Pontiac.

Doremus heard a grating noise and looked at the Chevelle. There was still smoke around it, as from burned brakes. The right-side door had opened and he saw a pair of hands, a stragly blond head. She came crawling determinedly out, stood up, wobbled, leaned against the roof of the Chevelle. She looked at the splintered fence and the rubble at her feet and then toward him, blindly. Doremus wondered how he could have forgotten all about Amy.

"Would somebody please help me?" she asked in a timid voice.

He was there in plenty of time to grab her before the wobble could get any worse.

Sixteen

THE SOFT SOUND OF THE SEA UNCURLING AGAINST THE NARROW strip of sand beach a few yards away from the honeymoon cottage awakened her, as it usually did, shortly after dawn. She floated, delightfully, for another ten minutes between sleep and full awareness before edging out of bed.

The air-conditioner was off but there was a slight chill in the bedroom and she remembered it had rained during the night. She stripped off the filmy trifle of nightgown in which she had slept, letting it drift to the rumpled king-size bed. She looked with a trace of a smile where Doremus had slept for a few hours before the thought of uncaught fish out there in the sea had raised him and sent him stumbling off in the black of night with half-opened eyes. She shook her head at this unshakable dedication and went into the bathroom for a five-minute shower.

Afterward, smiling to herself, she chose light-blue shorts and a bright Jamaica print blouse, dressed, slipped her feet into Italian sandals and went out on the porch. The sun was behind her, its heat not apparent yet, but the sky had turned blue. The precisely clipped grass of the lawn and the fronds of the two palms were still beaded from the rain. Out on the placid water there was a long low boat with two men in it. She thought she recognized her husband and smiled again.

When the two men were close to shore and she could see they had a catch, she ran past the little emerald-shaped swimming pool and went down to the beach. Doremus, wearing boat shoes, swim trunks and a straw hat, was in the water, helping the guide beach the boat.

"I thought you were sleeping late today," he said chidingly.

"Every intention; but there's something about the sound of the ocean; it can pry you out of the warmest bed." She nipped a kiss into his neck, pleased with the salt taste of his red-brown skin. In a week's time he had tanned marvelously, while she had been forced to sit on the porch in the shade, recovering from the folly of her initial day in the sun. He was also filling out, she noticed with satisfaction. There seemed to be some padding over his ribs. She pinched to make sure. He rubbed fish odor into her hair and she ducked away hastily, began uncovering their breakfast. There was a plate of fresh tropical fruit—papaya, melon, pineapple—two platters of ham and eggs, a large basket filled with muffins. And one little plate had two letters on it.

"Mail," she said, and sliced the envelopes open with a butter knife. She was reading when Doremus came back from washing up. He bent over nonchalantly to kiss a bare and somewhat flaky arm.

"Who's that one from?"

"Helen," she said.

He yawned, cracked his jaws, poured another cup of coffee.

"How's everything back in The Shades?"

"Normal," Amy said, absorbed in the letter. As she was reading, a wisp of shadow crossed her face. She put the letter down beside her plate and stared off toward the water. A man on horseback came along the beach, disappeared down the line of cottages.

"Something?" he said, after a while.

"Oh . . . no, it's all right." But she left the table and stood with her back to him.

"Peggy's all right, I hope."

"Yes, fine. They're all fine. They had a picnic the other day. The three of them—Helen, Peg and Peter. Helen says Peter is talking quite a lot now, when he forgets himself. That's usually when he's around Peg. When they're together they're in their own little world." Amy's head dropped slightly. "And we're . . . in our own little world, and I've never been happier, so why can't I forget about it, all of it? Am I going to be haunted the rest of my life, am I always going to get the shakes when I think of . . . Craig?"

Doremus put his napkin down thoughtfully, got up, guided her to the ornamental couch. "No, you aren't," he said. "Keep in mind that it's only been five months. Some kinds of shock don't wear off in a hurry. What you went through was the equivalent of a particularly nasty combat operation. There are men alive today still having nightmares about World War Two. Give yourself a little time, Amy. In our little world."

"I love you so very much, Doremus. I don't think you're ever off my mind. When you're out there in the dark fishing I get a little scared. Now it's fine. Now I feel even a little bit brave and confident. But I don't like for you to go away even for an hour. I'm talking like a—"

"A wife," he said. "What happened to the appetite?"

She looked at him sheepishly. "I've got a stupid question, as long as I'm in this mood. Then I'll shut up forever. Doremus . . . what made you pick me? I was sure you were in love with Helen. I thought I recognized all the symptoms. I had made up my mind. Amy's Blue Period. You were going to marry Helen. I was going to join the Salvation Army or something. Then, out of nowhere that afternoon, 'I think it's time to get married, Amy.'"

"Very romantic of me," he said, his lip curling. "As long as we're opening up, let me say I was scared stiff. I thought I was too old for you. I expected withering scorn."

"Anything but a blubbery face and a very delighted girl in your lap. Too old! When you're a hundred and nineteen I'll be a hundred and one. But you didn't tell me yet. Helen is a damned good-looking, mature and thoughtful woman. She has style and serenity. What did you want with me? It wasn't sympathy, was it?"

"Sure."

"Oh, thanks a lot!"

"I was feeling sorry for myself. Tossing in bed at night like a sixteen-year-old virgin. Fumbling around. Not eating right. I was very sorry for myself because you were on my mind, Amy. As you are now, as you always will be. And Helen wasn't."

She looked closely at his face, then nodded. "That simple, hey?"

"That's all there is to it. I loved Amy Lawlor and I'm glad I was man enough to tell her. Now I'm hungry enough to eat two breakfasts instead of one if you don't get over to the table before I do. And then I think when I'm chock full I'll wander down to the hotel and send a cable to Nelson in Chicago telling him that it'll be my pleasure to represent his fine detective agency in the city of San Francisco and to wire me a couple of thousand dollars care of Barclay's because I'm on my honeymoon and I want to treat my bride to a trunkful of new clothes. And then I think we ought to get in that little Ford out there and—"

"Whoa, whoa," Amy said quickly, kissing him. He held her very tightly and for quite a long time, and one of the tall hotel waiters walking by turned his head at such an angle he almost lost the tray he was toting.

"On second thought," Doremus said with vague smile, "I think I'll forget about the breakfast for now, and I can always send the wire this afternoon. Or some other time."

"Or some other time," Amy repeated, and obediently followed him into the shady cottage.

The Rebellion
of Yale Marratt
By Robert H. Rimmer

He took two wives and defied society to damn his morals

Robert Rimmer – author of the most controversial
bestseller of the decade THE HARRAD EXPERIMENT –
now turns his pen to the subject of bigamy. And tells
the story of one man's unconventional sexual behavour
which became a national controversy.

On its publication in America, Rimmer was publicly
condemned in several States and burned in effigy.

THE NEW ENGLISH LIBRARY 6s.

THE HARRAD EXPERIMENT

**The frank, provocative and controversial
best seller.**

by Robert H. Rimmer

A computer picked them as partners for free
love. Four hundred young men and women who
live, learn and love together at Harrad University—
the college of sexual freedom.

**There has never been an experiment like
Harrad before.**

There has never been a book like this before.

What is happening at Harrad?

THE NEW ENGLISH LIBRARY 6s.

NEL BESTSELLERS

Science Fiction

F.2658	GLORY ROAD	Robert Heinlein 7/6
F.2844	STRANGER IN A STRANGE LAND	Robert Heinlein 12/-
F.2630	THE MAN WHO SOLD THE MOON	Robert Heinlein 6/-
F.2386	PODKAYNE OF MARS	Robert Heinlein 6/-
F.2449	THE MOON IS A HARSH MISTRESS	Robert Heinlein 8/-
F.2754	DUNE	Frank Herbert 12/-

War

F.2423	STRIKE FROM THE SKY—THE BATTLE OF BRITAIN STORY	Alexander McKee 6/-
F.1686	EASTERN APPROACHES	Fitzroy Maclean 7/6
F.2645	THE LONGEST DAY	Cornelius Ryan 5/-
F.2146	THE LAST BATTLE (illustrated)	Cornelius Ryan 12/6
F.2527	A SOLDIER MUST HANG	J. D. Potter 5/-
F.2471	THE STEEL COCOON	Bentz Plagemann 5/-
F.2494	P.Q.17—CONVOY TO HELL	Lund Ludlam 5/-
F.1084	THE GUNS OF AUGUST—AUGUST 1914	Barbara W Tuchman 5/-

Western

F.2134	AMBUSH	Luke Short 3/6
F.2135	CORONER CREEK	Luke Short 3/6
F.2142	THE ALAMO	Lon Tinkle 3/6
F.2063	THE SHADOW SHOOTER	W. C. Tuttle 3/6
F.2132	THE TROUBLE TRAILER	W. C. Tuttle 3/6
F.2133	MISSION RIVER JUSTICE	W. C. Tuttle 3/6
F.2180	SILVER BUCKSHOT	W. C. Tuttle 3/6

General

F.2420	THE SECOND SEX	Simone De Beauvoir 8/6
F.2117	NATURE OF THE SECOND SEX	Simone De Beauvoir 5/-
F.2234	SEX MANNERS FOR MEN	Robert Chartham 5/-
F.2531	SEX MANNERS FOR ADVANCED LOVERS	Robert Chartham 5/-
F.2766	SEX MANNERS FOR THE YOUNG GENERATION	Robert Chartham 5/-
F.2136	WOMEN	John Philip Lundin 5/-
F.2333	MISTRESSES	John Philip Lundin 5/-
F.2382	SECRET AND FORBIDDEN	Paul Tabori 8/6
U.2366	AN ABZ OF LOVE	Inge and Sten Hegeler 10/6
F.2374	SEX WITHOUT GUILT	Albert Ellis Ph.D. 8/6
F.2511	SEXUALIS '95	Jacques Sternberg 5/-
F.2584	SEX MANNERS FOR SINGLE GIRLS	Dr. G. Valensin 5/-
F.2592	THE FRENCH ART OF SEX MANNERS	Dr. G. Valensin 5/-

Mad

S.3702	A MAD LOOK AT OLD MOVIES	4/6
S.3523	BOILING MAD	4/6
S.3496	THE MAD ADVENTURES OF CAPTAIN KLUTZ	4/6
S.3719	THE QUESTIONABLE MAD	4/6
S.3714	FIGHTING MAD	4/6
S.3613	HOWLING MAD	4/6
S.3477	INDIGESTIBLE MAD	4/6

NEL P.O. BOX 11, FALMOUTH, CORNWALL

Please send cheque or postal order. Allow 9d. per book to cover postage and packing (Overseas 1/- per book).

Name...

Address ....

....

Title ....
(JUNE)